D1021430

King

Tanya Chapman

Coach House Books, Toronto

first edition

Canadä

Published with the assistance of the Canada Council for the Arts and the Ontario Arts Council. We also acknowledge the Government of Ontario through the Ontario Book Publishing Tax Credit Program and the Government of Canada through the Book Publishing Industry Development Program.

LIBRARY AND ARCHIVES CANADA CATALOGUING IN PUBLICATION

Chapman, Tanya, 1971-
King / Tanya Chapman.

ISBN-13: 978-1-55245-173-1
ISBN-10: 1-55245-173-9

I. Title.

PS8605.H365K46 2006 C813'.6 C2006-905282-4

For Fraser, of course

It's been King and Hazel for months now, always together. King found me just after I found the trailer park. Or maybe it's the other way around. Maybe the park found me and I found King. Chicken and egg.

Our best friends are Spiney and Sissy – they live just down the road from us. King and Hazel and Spiney are all earned names, but Sissy is a given name. Sissy exactly fits her, not in a bad way like what the word means, but more how it sounds: *Sissy*. Sissy's parents smoked a lot of pot, so maybe they picked the name for the sound and not the meaning. Her mom was dosed on acid when Sissy was born, so Sissy isn't exactly like everyone else. The main thing about Sissy is that she talks – a lot.

Spiney got his name because he's the exact opposite of Sissy: quiet. His quietness comes off to strangers as cool and tough, but the truth is that he's a real softie. He wouldn't want anyone to know that, though. If he doesn't know the exact right thing to say, he doesn't talk at all. He just stands there and looks at everyone until someone else talks, usually Sissy. It makes everything that does come out of his mouth even better because you know that he figured it was worth saying.

And King got his name because he just is, well, King.

What I love best about the four of us is that we're happy just hanging out and being ourselves. It's always a good time when we go on a tear together.

Old Joe's is the only bar in town that isn't depressing in that fading, alcoholic kind of way, so we always end up there and we have a blast.

The bar is country – there are country songs on the juke and sawdust on the floor that might really be just covering a lot of dirt. There's neon beer signs hanging all over the place and a clock that runs backwards just to mess with your head. Country isn't really our thing, but we do it up anyway.

The greatest part of Old Joe's is Old Joe himself; he's one of the best guys in town. When we come in all grinning and ready for fun, he rolls his eyes and says, 'Here we go again,' and he starts pouring the beer. We don't have to order all night because when our glasses get low he's there with another jug. Sometimes he charges us and sometimes he doesn't. He says that we drink more in one night than the whole town does all week, so he can afford to share the wealth.

Old Joe says brilliant things like 'When there's no place else to go then you've found your home' and 'There's always a bit of truth in a lie but only for the teller.' He says the kinds of things that pop into your head later at the strangest times. And he tells us great stories about hunting and fishing and riding motorbikes across the country. King is all blown up about motorbikes – that's what he does, fixes motorcycles and lawn mowers and any other thing with an engine that can break. So when Old Joe starts in on a motorbike story, we can kiss King goodbye.

It's funny to see King and Old Joe talk to one another. You can tell by looking at them that they like each other. Old Joe tells me that King is a prince among men. King tells me that Old Joe is a sage and that you can figure out everything in the world just by talking to him about engines.

The four of us are great drinkers. We can drink anyone in town under the table. But King can top us all. He is always the last one standing, so he's in charge of the night. I come in second, though – a fact I'm very proud of. Even though I'm small, I can keep up pretty good. It's tough to drink like that. It takes diligence, concentration and daily training – not to mention the constitution of a Spartan soldier.

Sissy talks constantly whether she drinks or not. She is the most honest person I've ever met – you know she's really honest and it's not just a put-on because she says every little thing that comes into her head. You can't hide anything when you're running like that. I figure it has something to do with the acid birth. She talks so much that her voice is always low and raspy like a two-pack-a-day smoker. I've never seen her go very long without talking and I've never, ever seen her sit still. Most times I try and listen and say things back to her like 'Oh yeah' or 'Tell me about it.' But sometimes I get overloaded, and then I go into my own head for a while and just tune out and listen to the sound of her voice but not the words. She doesn't seem to mind.

I'm having a relaxing moment of tuning out when this drunk guy beside me stands up and yells, 'Wet T-shirt contest – yeehaw!' And sloshes a whole mug of beer down my front. I'm not sure if he meant to spill so much beer on me but I don't care. I stare at him, deciding on the best way to get my revenge, and then Sissy is back in focus, talking me down.

'And you know, Hazel,' she says, 'there's just nothing you can do with a person like that. You have to let it all roll because if you start letting those bad vibes come into your life, then you may as well give up now. You have to control everything around you so you can make your own life into what you want it to be.'

'Cheers, Sissy,' I say.

The only time Sissy shuts up is when you cheers her. She gives me a big smile and says, 'Cheers, baby,' and takes a drink. I cheers Sissy a lot. If I was as nice and as patient as Sissy, I would listen to her all the time, but I'm not, so I don't. So I cheers her and use the pause while she's drinking to get away from the wet T-shirt guy and look for King.

Everyone loves King, and King loves drinking games. So when he says, 'Let's play caps,' you can bet that everyone is in for the fun. Right now there are ten people sitting on the hardwood floor engaged in a caps tournament to the death. The idea is that you and your partner sit across from each other and set a beer cap upside down on top of your bottles, and then you take turns shooting caps at each other's bottle to try and knock off the cap. If someone knocks off your cap, you have to take a drink and they get another shot. The game is stupid easy. I guess all drinking games have to be stupid easy.

There's a specific tech to caps, a certain way to flick so that you have the aim and the force to take out the other person's cap. I never bothered to learn it so I don't play the game. King plays, though, and he's also the judge of the whole floor. People in caps disputes are always yelling, 'Hey, King, I think I should get another chance.'

And he yells at the top of his lungs, 'Do-over, baby!'

King's in a good mood tonight. When he's not in such a good mood, he yells, 'All's fair in love and caps, baby!' And there's no do-overs for anyone.

King's caps partner is this chick I've never seen before. She keeps grinning at him and making a pouty face like a baby when she misses. He's giving her more do-overs than anyone.

I walk right into the middle of their game and look down at King. He grins at me and says, 'How you doing, light of my life?'

'Just checking in.'

'You're a star.'

'I am,' I say and turn to look at the girl he's playing against. I telepathically beam my thought into her head – *Don't bother, don't even think about bothering*.

King goes back to playing caps and I walk far enough away to be out of the picture but still able to see the chick out the corner of my eye. She is too busy being swept off her feet by King to notice that I exist – so much for my powers of mind control. King doesn't mean to do it, but chicks just dig him. He's honest-to-god picture-book beautiful and, to top it off, he has this cool lopsided grin that's completely cowboy. He's a chick magnet. The broad sitting on the floor is hardly even bothering to play caps.

I've been staring at her staring at him for ten whole seconds. Ten seconds is a long time to be staring at someone. She's still doing it. Still. I'm wearing my big army boots and I think about how easy and fun it would be to just take a couple of steps over there and kick. But then I think of Sissy and how upset she would be, so I just walk away.

I go over and talk to some people I haven't seen since last time we were here. We dare each other into a line-dancing contest, this being a country bar and all. Some old-timey song starts up and we stand in a line in the middle of the dance floor. No one knows what the hell we're doing, but we have this whole fabulous routine. Step, step, turn, clap, one foot out, then the other foot out, turn and begin all over again. Sissy is right in the middle of things yelling out the moves and getting everything wrong. Spiney leans against the bar and pretends he doesn't know us, which is pretty hard because Sissy keeps yelling, 'Come on, Spiney – you taught me this one!' We dance the song and then we start over. By the second time through, everyone is busting a gut they're laughing so hard.

I'm caught up in step-step-turning and realize that line dancing is the best thing ever invented. The song ends and everyone looks at one another and starts laughing all over again. We all bow and curtsy and the guys act like old-school cowboys tipping their pretend hats and hitching their jeans.

I come out of a twirl and focus my eyes. King and the caps girl are standing now and she has her arm around his waist. King is talking to someone else and balancing a beer bottle on the open palm of his hand. He's acting like he doesn't notice.

Sissy sees me and stops smiling as she follows my eyes over to King. She walks towards me quickly. She has her quiet voice on because she knows that big trouble could start right now. She grabs my arm and steers me out of the bar, my army boots half dragging along the floor.

Sissy hauls me to the parking lot. 'You can't do that, Hazel. No matter what the world hands you – '

'I really don't care about the world right now, Sissy. I care that that chick is in there hanging off King.'

'If you give in to the bad vibes then you will be in a territory where only bad will – '

'Okay. Okay. Let's just get the hell out of here before I see her again.'

'There you go, Hazel. Take the situation into control and deal with it in a positive way so that – '

I stop listening because I've decided to go to the quarry. A swim in the quarry is always a good fix. We find the Duster and hop in. I know I shouldn't drive after so much beer, but goddamn I love it. I take paths through fallow fields. The tall grasses brush against the car windows and we roll them down to stretch out our arms and feel the damp, dark tops. The night air swirls in and around us and takes away the smoke and stale beer smells left over from the bar. We don't even turn on the radio.

When we get to the quarry, we strip down, throw our clothes on the hood of the car and run to the edge of the highest cliff. The gravel bites against my feet and wakes me up. Moonlight hits the limestone of the quarry on all sides, making it glow silvery white. I curl my toes against the side of the cliff and look down – I can't see a thing. Somewhere below us is water.

I look over at Sissy and stick out my tongue. She grins back and I put my finger to my lips. 'Shhhh.'

We jump.

Falling through the air in the dark is one of my favourite things to do. There's a point in your fall when you think that there's nothing below you. Maybe you'll never hit the water. Maybe you've already hit and you're dead. Then, just when you believe that it's all over, you land. All of a sudden you're alive, and whatever was getting you down is gone.

The force of the fall pushes me deep, and I let myself torpedo under for one powerful moment. No one knows how deep the quarry is. There are rumours of Mafia cars, dead bodies and stolen treasure hidden in this water.

A million bubbles swirl around me. When you jump from great heights you have to use bubbles to orient yourself because you can get confused and swim the wrong way – deeper instead of up. I follow the bubbles straight to the top, burst through to the air and take a deep breath. And there's Sissy grinning.

Then Sissy and I float. We are really great at floating. We can float forever. Naked floating combined with blind jumping can take away any trouble in the world. My ears are underwater and I can hear Sissy's muted words, her voice echoing softly between the limestone walls of the quarry. Sissy's voice, when you don't really have to listen, is a beautiful thing.

I came home in a great mood but now everything is wrong again. I'm walking around the trailer singing angry songs at the top of my not-so-puny voice, and I don't care who in this unglamorous place I wake up.

I don't make up words for songs very well when I'm drunk or angry, and now I'm both, so I'm singing 'What the hell is going on?' with 'It's all wrong, it's all wrong' as the chorus. Pretty stupid.

King's not home. That's what made everything bad again. I want to go back to the quarry, to be anywhere except here. I want to talk to Old Joe so he can tell me that something good will come out of this. But I can't think of a damn thing that Old Joe or anyone else could tell me to make this stupid situation even close to okay. I find King's guitar and take all the strings off, which is super-bad because it bends the neck. I twist the tuning heads and hear the notes go flat and then flatter and then wind themselves down to just plain noise. I look around for more destruction, but there's nothing else I can think to touch that would piss him off more. So I sit and try not to cry like a silly little girl.

I try not to think of King and the caps girl in some field somewhere doing god knows what. The more I try not to think about it, the clearer the scene becomes. I can practically hear every word they're saying from wherever they are.

I have to chill out, so I figure that this is as good a time as any to water the flowers. I go out to the back of the trailer, turn on the hose and get the spray gun. I think of the caps girl. I can't help it. I try to remember if she's pretty, if she's prettier than me. I think of King playing caps with her and the one time I saw him look at her. I try to analyze his face. But there is nothing in my memory. Their features turn into expressions that I can't figure out, knowing glances that I never saw. I wish I wasn't so drunk so I could remember if the looks really happened. Then again, I'm glad I'm drunk and wish I was drunker because the fact, the real fact, is that King isn't here – again.

I even went for a float first, and I still beat him home. That's a lot of time to play with, especially on a drunken night. I yank the hose to the front of the trailer and think violent King thoughts. I stand in the middle of the lawn, press the trigger on the spray gun and start weaving in a too-drunk-not-drunk-enough circle.

And then there's the top of King's head popping out of a patch of waist-high flowers. I have the gun spraying right against his chest, and he's soaked.

His voice is sleepy. 'Hey, Hazel, hey, what are you doing watering at this time of night?'

'I heard it's better to water at night.'

'Yeah, I think I heard that too.'

I haven't turned off the gun or moved my aim. The water is still spattering full blast against his T-shirt. He must be sitting in mud by now.

'Why don't you come over here?'

'Because it's wet over there. And I don't want to wreck my dress.'

So he stands up and walks right into the water with it soaking him even more, and he takes the gun out of my hand. Then he picks me up and takes me to a dry part of the flowers. We lie down on our backs, side by side, and stare up at the night.

'You know, Hazel, when you lie down here and all you can see is the top of the flowers and the stars, it's like we're the only two people in the world.'

'I wish we were … I wish the caps girl didn't exist in the world.'

'Ahh, the caps girl.'

'Why do you do it, King?'

At first, I think he's not going to answer or that he'll pretend he doesn't know what I'm talking about. I think if he does that, I might have to hit him. I've been waiting a long time, all night almost, to let the violence reign, and now I have the person who makes me the maddest in the world right here. But I have no chance.

'I don't know, I don't know anything. You just get so mad. Sometimes the biggest thing I do is make you mad. Sometimes I feel like I'm trying to exist and the only thing that reacts to my trying is you. Maybe you are the only one who knows that I'm here. I need to see that sometimes. You know?'

'Over and over?'

'Maybe.'

We lie there for a while. King smooths the hair from my forehead, and I can feel the anger leaving me with every stroke. I remind myself that he was here all the time. I remind myself that my anger is really all because of me. I relax and let King hold me and make me feel comfortable again.

'Hey, King, you know that girl who lives three doors down, she's kind of slow?'

'Yeah.'

'Well, she has a friend now.'

'Oh yeah?'

'They ride their bikes together. He comes by her house, waits in the driveway and rings the bell on his bike until she pokes her head out the front door. And then he says to her, "Want to go for a bike ride?" And she runs right out the door with two cans of pop that she's been holding behind her back since she heard his bell. She gives one to him, and they take off down the road together.'

'That's beautiful, Hazel.'

We look at the tops of the flowers and the stars for a while.

'You know, Hazel, there's this girl who wears flowered dresses all the time, even in winter, because she wants to bring a little something magical into the trailer park where she lives. Only, I want to tell her that there's always a little something magical following her around whatever she wears. And sometimes when I look at her, I can't believe that she's with me. It's like I have to shake it into myself. And when talking to her and touching her doesn't make her any more real, I have to wreck shit up so that I can watch the fury and know that she cares about what I'm doing. It's a shitty way to go, but sometimes I think it's the only thing I've got.'

'Does that mean you're sorry?'

'Only if you're sorry for whatever it was I heard you do to my guitar.'

'I don't know if I'm sorry for that yet.'

'Close enough.'

He laughs and holds me tighter, and we fall asleep in the flowers.

King and I live in the Evening and Morning Star Trailer Park. There is a sign above the entrance of the park that spells out EVENING AND MORNING STAR TRAILER PARK in wooden letters. Or used to spell it out – half of the letters have fallen into the ditch so that now the sign just says EVEN MOR T ARK. The creepy thing is that if you know a bit of French then you can see that the sign says EVEN DEATH ARK, which makes me think of a Noah and a million doomed animals. But I don't want to think of a Death Ark every time I come home, so we just call it EVEN MORE, as in even more fun and even more life.

King is not King's real name and Hazel is not my real name, but that's what everyone calls us. We live in a trailer park and not a real nice one either. But this is the park that found me by fate so this is the park that belongs to me.

I remember exactly what happened the day I found Even More. I was driving down the road in my '71 Duster. I had nothing to do and nowhere to go and I was getting a full dose of that real and true freedom. I had been driving around for two weeks already looking for I don't know what, and I was getting kind of tired and excited like I might be close to the end of my trip. I had a feeling that anything could happen and I was ready for it. Do you turn at the next crossroads or go straight? And then what? You turn one way and you become one sort of person, turn the other way and you become another. Who knows? The freedom is that it's all up to you.

And that's how I found this place. I stopped here. I was tired of driving away from things and not towards anything in particular and I was ready to take a break and then there it was: Even More. Right in the middle of nowhere, just sitting there ready to be found. And in front of the park was the trailer, my trailer, with a For Sale sign stuck on the door. Well, how can you turn your back on that?

There's some cool people here but there could be more flowers on front lawns, if you know what I mean. I wear a dress every day to combat the lack of glamour, and I have a fantastic repertoire of hairstyles. Last week I discovered liquid eyeliner. Much better than the crayon kind, so every day I wear a little bit more. I can't help it. It's an unstoppable beauty progression.

Today I'm doing my magic on the flowers since I didn't really get to water them properly last night. I have the most flowers in the park, which isn't much of a challenge, but I have *by far* the most flowers in the park. I like the wild kind.

I found these wildflower seeds that come from Newfoundland. Newfoundland flowers grow everywhere, they're not picky – they'll even grow in ditches and other places where they should never be able to survive. I admire them for that, so I bought fourteen packages and scattered them out front. So now the whole yard looks like a Newfoundland ditch.

You have to walk right through the flowers to get to the door – I never thought of a path. The flowers are almost three feet high so you can't step around them – you have to walk right through. But you don't have to worry that you're going to crush them, because they'll just keep on living no matter how often you go to the door.

My favourite thing to do is sing and water the flowers. I love how the sun hits the shoots of water from the spray gun and makes little rainbows. Everything is shiny. The spray gun is one of the best things around the house. I've got a sprinkler, the kind that goes back and forth and makes little waterfalls, but I love the gun because it gives me total control. I can get every last flower and not worry that the sprinkler has left anyone out. King got me the sprinkler and the gun. Every time he's in the hardware store he looks for a new water toy for me. I've got about ten different kinds of sprinklers in a pile out back. That's the kind of guy King is: if he knows you like something, he can't stop himself from getting it for you.

Sometimes I water too much. I can't help myself. I just kind of zone out and go somewhere else for a while. I get lost in all that water. It's like almost remembering something – like that feeling when a name is on the tip of your tongue or like you are just one teensy mental jump away from a really great discovery. It's that feeling exactly. The great idea hovers in front of you like a bubble and if you are ever going to understand it properly you have to climb on inside. And that's where I get lost.

One time King came home and found me standing in a lawn full of mud. I was just turning around very slowly, watching the spray. He said he waded through the lawn, eased my fingers off the water gun, unwound me from the hose and carried me inside. I was soaked and covered in mud and humming some tune. But I don't remember any of that. He said I just smiled and touched his face and went to sleep.

We figured out later that I was watering for two hours. The next morning, I was sad because I had trampled some of the flowers and also because I lost the discovery and the day. The losing-time thing happens now and then. Once I went out for a walk and never turned around to come home. King found me on the side of the highway. It was no big deal, but I wish I could remember those big ideas that I get stuck inside – you could change the world with a discovery like that.

King said that when he found me on the lawn soaked and humming, standing in a pile of mud and hose, it was the most beautiful thing he had ever seen. So I guess it was okay to lose a couple of flowers and some time.

Some people would freak if they saw their old lady soaked and whacked out in the front yard or on the side of the highway, but that's why I love King like I do: when everything in the world is crazy he's just like the water – shiny.

My neck won't move so I can't look left, and right isn't much good either. That's what I get for napping on the couch. But the neck thing will go away. The thing that won't go away is that King didn't sleep here last night. Not on the couch or anywhere else in the trailer. I sit for a while not thinking about the caps girl.

And then, before I have time to do much more worrying, King is at the door looking godawful, half walking half stumbling into the trailer. He slumps down on the rocker to tell me the whole story. Last night he was in jail. Nothing serious, a B & E that was more like trespassing.

King likes to go to this old gravel pit with Spiney. King and Spiney used to be in a rock band together. There's great acoustics in the pit, so they climb over the fence and scream their heads off, making the sounds of all the instruments and singing the mostly forgotten words to all their old songs.

I heard it once. In a small town you can hear just about everything. Listening to them in the pit going off like banshees made me want to scream along with them, scream out loud for all the times I couldn't make any noise at all and scream for the times I thought it would be better not to – there are a million reasons for screaming once you get going.

When King and Spiney are on a rage in the pit, it doesn't take long for the cops to collect them and throw them in jail for the night. So if they don't wrap up their screaming and get out pronto, then that's what always happens, and they end up in the drunk tank. But they've never had to stay the whole night before. King is a natural charmer, so usually when they get thrown in jail King starts talking and convinces the cop on duty to let them go. That's another small-town thing, I guess: eventually you meet all the cops. They start talking about the old days and the band and next thing you know King is a free man.

That's how it usually goes, but last night they had to stay. No amount of charm could get him home.

Today, after jail, King must have gone over to Spiney's trailer and tried to drink away the night. He's home now, but it's only four in the afternoon and he's already on a rant about being the victim of crazy mindless rules and how it all sucks. This is the ten-beer rant, so I figure he's been drinking for a while. My guess is that the boys went straight to the beer store as soon as they got let out this morning. So right now King is sitting on the rocking chair in our little trailer living room, but he sure isn't rocking.

'Hazel,' he says, 'you know there's only so much a person can do to have fun, and when you run out of ideas there's only trouble.'

'There's only trouble everywhere, King.'

'Yeah, you're right, but sometimes you can stay out and it's all okay. It's times like this that come around and ruin everything.'

'You crossed into trouble way back, and sometimes you jump back to the normal and somewhat boring side of things, but then you always go back to the crazy side.'

'I have to go back, Hazel.'

'I know you do. You just have to keep testing that line.'

'Yeah.'

'Can't let it get too far away.'

'Like you.'

King can hardly see because the cops maced him. I'm surprised about the police using mace on him but I don't say a thing. So while we're talking down the night, he's kind of crying. He keeps telling me it's just the mace. There's a tear on his cheek, and I wipe it off with the bottom of my dress. King puts his hand on my hair and pulls me into him.

I try to imagine my King in jail. Not jail where he probably knows the guards, but real jail. The Big House. Even one night seems impossible. He is so huge and free. I can't picture him in a little room made of concrete and bars like you see in the movies. In my mind, King couldn't possibly fit in a space like that.

Sometimes, like now, it feels as though even the whole big world isn't big enough for King.

I close my eyes and lean against him for a second, and when I open them again I see the blood. 'They got you good, King.'

'Absolutely shit-kicked,' he says and grins.

'What did you do?'

'They said I was being aggressive.'

I shake my head and look to the corner of the kitchen at my fish mobile. It's a ratty thing at first sight – little coloured glass fish tied to chopsticks with fishing line – but if you take the time to look at it and see it in just the right way, you can believe that you are underwater so completely that you hold your breath.

I go to the bathroom for peroxide and bandages to clean him up. The cuts are on his head, elbow and knees and down his leg. I wipe as gently as I can. There's lots of dirt and tiny pieces of gravel mixed with the dried blood. I start to worry a bit, wondering how much damage the cops did and how much he did himself. I wonder how serious a B & E can get, but I don't say anything out loud. It wouldn't be right to bring out my worry, not now. King would just tell me it was nothing, no matter what, and that everything was going to be okay. Even with his previous charges piling up on top of this new one. But the previous charges and the piling are another thing not to think about. The mobile spins slowly, and the fish swim and swim.

I use the bubbly peroxide and a cotton ball to wipe carefully, not wanting to cause more hurt. Maybe it's because I don't say my thoughts out loud that the worry settles in me. I can feel it deep in my chest and somewhere in the bottom of my stomach.

He reads my mind. 'I don't think this is all from the cops, Hazel. I was doing some damage before they got us.'

'Ripping it up,' I say and I smile because I can tell he's kind of proud of himself.

'Damn right,' he says. 'So now I have to go to court.'

I close my eyes and swallow down the bad thoughts.

'Damn,' I say. 'Court is always so early in the morning. No jail, though, right?'

'Nah, they won't put me in jail.'

'Because, you know, I can deal with a lot of things … '

'Yeah, I know,' he says. 'You can deal with anything but jail.'

I stand up and sit King straight in the rocking chair. I bow to the invisible judge sitting on the couch and pace the courtroom. 'Is this the kind of person you want to lock up, sir? Sure, he was screaming at the moon, but if this guy wants to throw himself down a gravel pit, why should we care? And besides, Your Judgementalist, he'll keep it down next time.'

I curtsy to the judge and smile at King.

'Hazel, you're hired.'

'Better than the guy they'll give you anyway,' I say.

'Better than anything.'

He pulls me into his lap and we rock back and forth for a while and talk about the fun parts that happened last night. King and Spiney always have a good time together – they can hang out for days on end without getting sick of each other. King tells me about how he almost wrote a song while they were in the pit. He was singing something that could be a really good bass line and wishes he could remember it.

And then we fall asleep. We sleep despite the cuts and the worry and the mace and the worry. When we're together we can sleep anywhere, at any time, under any circumstance. That's the kind of people we are.

Some people understand that life is supposed to be fun and some people don't. Eventually the ones who don't understand just get mean about it.

Like the time I was writing a cheque in the grocery store and the cashier asked my name because I was new in town, and I told her it was Hazel, and she said, 'Your driver's licence doesn't say Hazel.' I told her that I was finished with the other name, so now it's Hazel. Then, when I was leaving, she said goodbye and called me by my old name, real loud and with a nasty snarl in her voice. I had already written my legal name on the cheque so everything was legit. There was no reason for it. Just this 'I'm right and you're wrong' idea that you're not allowed to change things around and make things better for yourself.

I know King understands, though. He understands in the most complete way. And when I figured that out, I knew I loved him for good.

Sissy introduced me to King. She knocked on my trailer door two days after I moved in and invited me over for a beer. I spent the whole afternoon listening to her voice. King and Spiney came home from the shop where they work together and the four of us talked, played cards and had a darn good time. Pretty soon it was a ritual.

A couple of weeks later I invited King over for dinner. Sissy gave me the idea when she told me that King was living in the shop where he worked. I figured that a home-cooked dinner might be a pretty good evening for us. I needed to give him a chance to tell me that he liked me – it was obvious already.

Sissy came over that day to cook for me. I can't cook a thing except Kraft Dinner and grilled cheese, but King didn't know that back then. While Sissy was cooking, I decided that the trailer needed a bit of decorating, so I got out my collection of Christmas lights. The first week I was in town I got a job at the thrift shop. They were throwing out this huge box of lights – apparently, no one buys used Christmas lights. I hung up my whole collection – some on the front door, then on the whole front of the trailer. I just couldn't stop. King was coming over.

It was the best dinner. We went through three bottles of red wine and sat and talked all night. There was a lot of laughing and a lot of telling silly stories and making fun of one another. I almost forgot about the lights, but then I jumped up, so quickly it made my drunken head spin, and I grabbed King and led him out the front door.

I made him stand in the middle of the lawn with his eyes closed while I ran and plugged in the lights.

'Ta da!'

He almost fell over, he was so blown away at the sight. I went and stood beside him and looked. We stood for a while just staring. The whole trailer kind of glowed, like one of those super-coloured cartoons about nuclear reaction. So many colours all on top of each other and shining away in the warm night. Then King took my hand and put it on his chest, over his heart. 'Thanks, Hazel,' he said.

And there I was, standing in the hazy, many-coloured night feeling the beat of King's heart.

And that was it. We knew from then on that we understood each other, and we've never talked about it since. It's not really something you can say out loud anyway.

I work at the thrift shop in town. Lots of people get their noses all up in the air about second-hand stuff. Some people never want anything that's second-hand. They judge the store right away – I can see them through the big front window looking in and thinking that nothing is good enough. It's a very specific expression and it looks the same on everyone: like a sour-lemon face just underneath their normal walking-down-the-street face. When they see me looking back at them from the other side of the window, I get the look too, like I'm second-hand.

This is new to me – no one looked at me like that in my old life. But now I'm getting used to it, almost. I do live in a trailer park, after all. People don't see the real personalities in the park, or the great things in the shop, or me – just the trailers and a bunch of things that someone didn't want anymore.

King likes the fact that he fixes used cars and equipment and I sell used everything else. He says it's like we are keeping things alive together, giving second chances.

The thrift is only open four days a week so I don't make a lot of money, but I'm not exactly living the high life. Four days pays the bills and puts some fun on the table.

The thrift is a small operation owned and run by the town council. There's me and then there are the twins who take care of the money and report to the council. The twins are old ladies about seventy-nine years old and they're dotty. I mean, they are great and sweet and everything, but I have no idea how they manage to balance the books because they can't even keep their place in a conversation.

But the twins are just another thing that I like about working at the thrift.

On the days the thrift is closed, people leave their donations in a big wooden box out back. It's my job to haul it all inside, sort it, price it and hang it up. I also have to keep the place looking halfway decent, which is harder than it sounds because it's so crowded and generally down-at-the-heels.

Another good thing about this job is that I get the first look at all the stuff that comes in. The other week there was a huge bag full of belts. An entire bag. Who has that many belts to throw away? Leather, elastic, chain-link, rope: there was everything that anyone has ever thought to make a belt out of. I'm not a belt person myself, but I picked out a tough-looking one for Spiney, leather with a huge buckle. He wears it all the time.

The worst days are when a whole truckload of things comes in from one person, usually an old man or lady. You know right away what happened.

Sometimes the clothes don't have anything to say for themselves – they are just a collection of pants and shoes and shirts. But other times you can read a person's whole life.

Today is a day like that. There are nine huge plastic bags filled with dresses, great dresses with sparkle and glamour built right in. I lay them on the counter. There are tons of them. There are so many dresses that when I get them all out of the bags I can't find enough room to lay them all out straight. So I drape them over racks and along shelves, covering the whole place. After a while the shop starts to look like something else, something a little more beautiful. Who was this person? There sure isn't anywhere around here to wear these gowns. This lady must have been living in her own piano-bar-and-martini world.

I sit for a while and look around. The light comes in the big window and reflects off the sequins and the shine of the dresses. The whole place sparkles. I watch as the shine makes its way around the place, seeping into the dreariness and lighting things up a little.

The bell above the front door rings and a lady comes in. 'Holy crap,' she says and waves her hand at the dresses. Then she goes to the back of the shop to where the books are. This town is too small for a public library, so people are always coming in to pick up a paperback for twenty-five cents, fifty cents for a hardcover. She finds a Harlequin and leaves.

I take the dresses one by one and hang them carefully on a rack. They're heavy, so I have to use the best hangers. I go to gather up the bags that they came in and that's when I notice that there's a smaller bag that I haven't unpacked yet. I can feel beads and stones through the plastic. I pry open the knot that holds the bag closed and dump everything onto the counter.

We have a whole section of junk jewellery in the thrift shop. There are bead necklaces and fake gold brooches that look like jumping leopards or flying parrots. There are clip-on earrings made of plastic pearls and thin silver bracelets that turn your wrist green. But there's nothing like this.

I can't believe it when I take the jewellery out of the bag. It's spectacular. There are bobbles for every part of your body. They are all rich deep colours to go with the dresses. No cheap stuff here. No falling-apart strands of plastic beads, just loads of sparkle.

I fasten a big bracelet around my wrist. It's heavy, with glass stones cut to look like gems. My wrist looks different. I know I'm just Hazel standing in the middle of the thrift, but I don't quite feel that way anymore.

And that's when it hits me. I'm going to redecorate the shop. The place is pretty depressing, to tell the truth. A room full of unwanted things. But it doesn't have to be that way. After all, one person's trash is another person's treasure and all that.

The first thing I do is go to the back and see what kind of cleaning supplies the twins have stashed away. There's a big bottle of floor polish, so I haul all the racks to one side of the shop and clean half the hardwood floor. The results are pretty good. By the time I push everything to the other side and do the other half, it's looking better. I prop the front and back doors open so the place can air out. The smell of second-hand stuff clears and now everything smells like pine. The shiny floor perks the place up, gives it a bit of hope.

Every now and then someone walks into the shop. I tell them to go ahead and look around, that I'm just doing some spring cleaning. The real thrift shoppers don't mind cramped racks and messy piles – they're used to going through the jumble, hunting for that one perfect thing.

I move the racks around and box up some of the stuff that isn't likely to sell: clothes with missing buttons or stains. By the time I take all the wrecked clothes away, there's room for some of the better stuff to be seen. I organize by season and colour. I make the shop look more like a place where second-hand things won't be given the lemon face. I even make a window display.

Usually the window is the spot where things get put when you don't know what else to do with them. Kind of like the lost and found of the lost. But not anymore. I put all that junk in the back and make a display by hanging up my favourite of the glamorous dresses. I don't have a mannequin or anything, so I improvise. The ceiling is made of the kind of tile where you can push up a section and then loop a string around the bracket that the tile sits in. I put the dress on a hanger and then suspend it from the ceiling. Then I accessorize. I tie some bracelets and necklaces with fishing line and hang them so that they dangle somewhere around where wrists and a neck might be. This is a lot harder than it sounds. It takes a while and tons of adjustments.

But finally I go out to the sidewalk to judge the effect. If you look at the display really quickly, you almost think that there is a lady standing there. Now she needs a partner, so I find a suit and do the same hanging-up trick. I stand back and watch them. They don't have a care in the world. They're just standing around letting time go by. Maybe they're talking – having a vodka twist and smiling about the weather.

It took me my entire day, but the shop finally looks like it might have something to offer. I turn the radio on – it's stuck on an oldies station but that's just fine with me: 'Oh oh oh the charms about you will carry me to heaven.' I drag an old fan from the back and aim it at the people in the window so when I turn it on the breeze spins them. They're dancers now. Wrists and waists twirl around.

A lady comes into the shop and eyes the jewellery that I left on the counter.

'What a load of junk.'

I show her the bracelet on my wrist, letting the light reflect off the gems. 'This came in the same batch,' I say.

She laughs. 'Good god. I haven't seen stuff like that since my great-grandmother died.'

She quickly selects three paperbacks from the stack and hands me seventy-five cents. Then she picks up a handful of the jewellery and lets it fall through her fingers with a clatter. 'Remember when you were so young that you thought these things were real?' She laughs and I watch the jewellery fall on the counter. A ruby-and-diamond earring bounces off the register and hits the floor. 'Oh, sorry,' she says. But she isn't.

The lady stuffs the books in her purse and leaves. The bell above the door rings on her way out. I find the lost earring and hold it up to the light, all sparkle and no damage done.

I bring one of the dresses home and wear it around the trailer. When King sees me, he bows. All night he speaks in different accents, calls beer champagne and me his little chandelier.

Sissy and I are sitting at the kitchen table in her trailer. Sissy and Spiney's trailer looks a lot like mine except it's tidier. Sissy tries to make it look nice by buying new things for it all the time. Her idea of a new thing is anything that looks like it should be part of the space program, like the silver salt and pepper shakers on the black-topped glass table or the clock that looks like it should have hands but really it's digital. My trailer looks pretty much like it did when it was new in the sixties. I figure, why mess with a good thing?

When I say that Sissy is *mostly* a never-ending talker, it's because some days – days like this – she hardly talks at all. She gets depressed. Depressed like she doesn't want to get out of bed. And on days like this she needs me. Not that I can solve any of her problems, but I can convince her to get out of bed and make me a cup of tea. And that's more than she'd do otherwise. Spiney is no good for her in these times. He just gets frustrated or gets all over her, trying to make her feel better.

Also – and here's the kicker – it makes Sissy feel better to ask people the questions they don't want to ask themselves. I think she likes to see them squirm. It's like she's feeling so crappy that she wants to make other people feel bad too, just so she won't be alone with her sadness. This is the only time that Sissy can be mean.

But it's not really her asking the questions, not the Sissy that we know and love – it's someone else. It creeps in, and you can't really do anything about it except wait it out and love her despite the meanness. So I volunteer for the hot seat every time. Spiney can't handle that either – the hot seat, I mean.

'Hazel, why don't you learn how to cook?'

'It's too late for me, Sissy.'

'It's never too late, that's dumb. What do you think a stove is for anyway?'

'A place to set your drink when there's too many empties on the counter?'

She doesn't like that, so she just stares at me and waits for me to say something serious. But as much as I love Sissy, I'm just not prepared to tell her I've never even seen the inside of my oven. King does all the cooking and she knows it. So I drink my tea, which makes me think of the word 'teetotaller, teetotaller' over and over and wait for the next question.

'Don't you think that King has slept with lots of girls like the one he played caps with at Old Joe's?'

I can't let my hurt show or she will be on this topic all day. So I just sit and think of 'teetotaller' again. But, of course, I'm also wondering just how many caps girls he really did sleep with. But then for my own sanity I decide that it doesn't matter since we got that all worked out anyway. I just nod at Sissy and sit very quietly and wait.

Finally. 'Hazel, don't you want to have kids? What are you going to do when you have kids? You have to cook something then, you know.'

Sissy knows damn well that I don't want any kids. But Sissy wants kids, a lot of them. The thing is, she can't have them. I chalk it up to her acid birth. But now I know what's bothering her. When she gets down it's either the kid thing or she thinks that there are too many bad vibes floating around her and she can't get away – even if she runs real fast in her head. Her words, not mine.

So now that I know it's the kid thing, I know the cure. I drag Sissy to the Duster and head down to the farmers' market. Sissy loves the market, she's crazy for it. This is our third trip since I've known her. So far she has picked up two albino rabbits, a giant guinea pig and a turtle that now has its own little swimming pool. Sissy's yard is really crowded, but a cure is a cure. So we go to the farmers' market.

The drive to the market is quiet. We don't say much of anything until I pull into the dusty parking lot. Then I say, 'There sure are a lot of things here that are going to die if some-one doesn't take care of them.'

Sissy's eyes get really wide. 'No. Do you think someone will kill them?'

'For sure. Doomed.'

I hate to say stuff like this, but it has to be done. Our conversation is like this routine that we pretend we've never been through before. And besides, like I say, a cure is a cure.

'Oh god, Hazel, do you think Spiney would be mad if I brought home just one thing?'

'Well, maybe if it isn't too big.'

'Yeah, something little.'

'How can he argue if it's just little?'

So we walk around the farmers' market for about an hour. Sissy gets really serious when she's making this decision. All these animals depend on her. Maybe not really, but today, in Sissy's head, she is definitely saving a life. We walk all the way through the market and back again.

I keep Sissy away from the horses and the cows because they really are beautiful, and I know she would want to take one home and that just wouldn't do. As it is, every time Spiney sees us coming home from the market he looks at me like *Oh no, Hazel, not again*. But then he's happy because her crazy mood has passed. That's just like Spiney: he wants everything to be okay, whatever it takes. Even if he has to live in a zoo.

They sell everything at the market. There's cotton candy and dishcloths right beside pigs. Then on the other side of the pigs are sausages cooking on a grill. The pigs don't seem to mind. There are also a million gadgets and fun things to look at, like old-fashioned radios and china teacups. And right beside those things are Kiss the Cook aprons and some crazy pens that light up and play a tune when you write with them. It's like the market can't make up its mind which century it's in.

After a while of walking back and forth, Sissy sees this old farmer guy sitting on the tailgate of a dusty pickup. She goes over to him and looks in the back of the truck to see what he's selling. As soon as I see her face, I know that this is the saved life.

'A chicken, Sissy?'

'Chickens are little.'

'Yes, yes they are.'

So she buys a chicken and a big wire cage that she can set up in her yard. I buy six bulbs of flowers that bloom in the fall. We carry everything back to the Duster.

Sissy is ecstatic.

I want the chicken to go in the trunk, but she insists on putting it in the back seat so she can put the seat belt around the cage. And when Sissy smiles and says 'pleeease' like she's doing right now I can't say no.

'You did a good thing today, Sissy.'

'I love that chicken already.'

'What's it called?'

'Buck, of course.'

'You're real awful with names, Sissy.'

'It runs in the family.'

She gives me another big grin, and me and Sissy and Buck and six fall-blooming bulbs head home.

When we get to the trailer, King and Spiney are waiting for us, ready to take the second shift in case Sissy was still in a mood. King has bought all kinds of ice cream treats. We eat Drumsticks as Spiney sets up the cage for Buck and Sissy gives us all a running narration on the proper care and maintenance of chickens.

Spiney is so glad to have Sissy back to normal that you would think he was happy to have that mangy chicken show up.

King holds his Drumstick up for a cheers and says, 'Nice work, Hazel.'

'As Old Joe says,' I quote, 'there's nothing a little bit of sweetness can't fix.'

I'm rearranging the thrift again. A bunch of half-filled buckets of paint just came in. Not bad colours either. I'm way at the back where I stuck everything I didn't want to deal with on my last cleanup day. I'm trying to figure out how much of a pain it would be to paint the whole back wall. There's nothing like a good coat of paint to give a place a lift. I'm looking around to see if there's something to make shelves out of when there's a knock on the front counter.

'Hi there!' I have to yell because I'm crouched under a cabinet trying to see if I can take it apart.

'Hi.'

I can hardly hear the voice because it's so soft. The 'hi' sounds more like a question than a greeting. I crawl out and make my way to the front. There's a guy standing there. He's looking at everything except me – like he's here to inspect the premises. He's about my age, maybe a bit older.

'You moved everything.'

'Yep.'

He looks under the racks. 'And cleaned the floors.'

'Yep.'

'I like the window,' he says and walks out the door.

I look at the doorway and wonder who I just met, and then he's back again, standing in the doorway.

'You didn't get rid of the records, did you?'

'Nope.'

'How about all those boxes of electrical stuff?'

'Nope. Are you trying to find something that I moved? I can probably remember where it is.'

'Oh,' he says, and for the first time he looks at me. 'Sorry,' he says in an embarrassed way. 'I just like this place. It always has everything that I need.'

'You can say that again,' I smile. 'I'm Hazel.' I stick out my hand. We shake.

'Egbert,' he says.

'You're joking.'

'No, I wish I was, joking, I mean, I wish I was joking,' he laughs.

When he laughs he looks a lot less like a concerned inspector and more like an interesting person. I notice that his pants are too long and hemmed with staples – I like him more.

'I'm glad you like the window,' I say, and I tell him about the garbage bags of clothes and the sour-lemon faces and how I'm trying to fix the place up.

He tells me about going back to university in the fall, and that this is another lazy summer at home with absolutely nothing to do. 'Usually I poke around here and find something interesting to keep me occupied. Last year it was photography – I think I bought every camera in the place.'

'You want some tea?'

'You can make tea in here?'

'Sure, why not? You would be surprised at the stuff that's in here.'

'I doubt it.'

'Oh yeah,' I say and laugh.

He still looks like he might go but he manages to get himself the rest of the way in the door. 'Sure, sounds good. The tea, I mean.'

I plug in the kettle and Egbert looks at this strange metal contraption that he found on a shelf somewhere. It looks like a flask covered with leather, but it's not a flask. It's a box filled with something, but I could never figure out how to open it so I just threw it on a shelf and put a five-dollar tag on it.

'What is this?'

'Can I call you Egg?'

'Gross, but yeah.' He shakes the metal flask thing. 'So what is it?'

'Well, Egg, no one knows.'

'Really?' He shakes it again and looks for a latch.

'I've tried.'

'Weird.' He turns it upside down and shakes it some more, squinting his eyes and wrinkling his nose. When he's thinking about something and not being self-conscious he's pretty cute.

'Yeah. So what do you do anyway?' I pull two chairs from the back and set them up by the register so that they face each other. They're comfortable.

'What do I do?'

'Oh, come on,' I say. 'I'll go first. Mostly I work here and I like to garden and go to Old Joe's and hang out with my friends and sometimes I write songs but I don't really play guitar. And that's what I do. So what do you do?'

'Oh, well, I'm good at math. I'm taking business and computers at school.'

'What else?'

'Well, I don't go to Old Joe's because I don't drink.'

'Really?'

'Yeah. Is that strange?'

'No.' The kettle is ready so I get up and put the tea bags in the pot. 'So, what else?'

'Hmmm, well, I guess I help my dad a lot.'

'And what does Mr. Egg need help with?'

'He's the mayor – so mostly I just answer phones and talk nicely to people.'

'Do you like politics?'

'Don't know really. With a name like Egbert I can't exactly see myself winning friends and influencing people.'

'Yeah, well, I have freckles.'

'So?'

'And I had buckteeth.'

'Yeah?' He's sounding a little more hopeful.

'Buckteeth and freckles at least equals a bad first name. At least equal if not worse.'

'True, I feel so much better,' he says and grins.

Egg and I talk about the thrift and what I do all day and what I have tucked away in the back. Then we talk about computers and business and how they go together. It seems like we could go on and on with the conversation. It's like once we get started there's no stopping us. But eventually Egg stands up and says he has to get going. Then he fishes five bucks out of his pocket. 'I have to have this,' he says and holds up the boxy thingamajig that he was playing with.

'Okay, good luck with it,' I say.

Egg starts making his way to the door. 'You too.'

'With what?'

'Oh, I guess I meant bye.'

'Okay, bye. And Egg?'

He pokes his head back through the door. 'Yeah?'

'You can come back here any time you want.'

He smiles and nods and he's out the door. But then he pokes his head back in and says, 'Thanks for the tea, Hazel.' He gives one of those big smiles that he has and he's gone again.

I meet people at the bar, but those are drinking buddies. Drinking buddies are not friends – there's a definite line that drinking buddies don't cross. For instance, drinking buddies don't see each other during the day and drinking buddies don't make too many serious comments without throwing in a joke. You never really know them and they never really know you. And then I realize that the whole time Egg was here I didn't even think about court.

Some days in life are really beautiful and all you have to do on those days is walk around and love everything you see. Sissy says that there isn't nearly enough love in the world, but then that's just the kind of thing that someone like Sissy would say. When someone says something that sounds like how they look, it's best never to listen.

The sun is out and everything is dusty in the way that things can be dusty only after days and days of no rain. There's no work today, so I walked all morning with no place to go. I went by the quarry and followed some little trails in high grass that I never noticed before. I thought I might walk into town and go to Old Joe's and make him come out in the sunlight and see just how great the day is. Then I thought of drinking and thought that there's lots of time for that later. So I just kept wandering and halfway there I knew I was going to see King at work.

King works in a little garage on the outskirts of town. Just where nothing turns into even more of nothing. So I walked there, but as I got closer I knew that I didn't want to talk to King. I just wanted to know that he was in the world on a day like this, just to make things perfect for myself.

That's where I am now, sitting in the ditch across the road from the shop, leaning against a pole watching King and Spiney fix a bike. I love to watch the guys do things like this, all their thoughts wash over their faces. Sometimes King even talks to the thing he's working on, almost purrs to it – like 'Come on, come on' – to coax it into being fixed. Right now he's reaching right into the guts of an engine and looking up at the sky like he can see up there the things that his hands can feel.

King is in the world, I say to myself and I can't help but smile.

In one week, King is going to court, and I think that if the judge could only see him working right now, then everything would be okay for us. Then immediately I try to get the court thought out of my head.

But the thought is like a fly landing on a piece of flypaper. You put the paper out to catch the flies, but then one lands and you feel kind of bad for it, just stuck there like that. You wish you'd never bought the damn flypaper in the first place. But now everything is wrecked and you're the one who did it.

I glance up to see King and Spiney look at the bike and then frown at each other. King lights a cigarette and they stand there together shaking their heads and staring. I sneak out of the ditch and head home. I don't want King to know that I'm watching him. It seems wrong, all of a sudden, to spy on them. When I get back to the main road I feel like I've escaped something.

Sometimes your memory takes a picture of a person. You never know when it's going to happen. But forever after that moment, you think of that person and up pops this one picture. All the way home, I think of King looking up into the sky with his hands on the broken bike saying, 'Come on, come on,' like he's praying. Then I realize that King can probably fix anything that has ever been broken. I realize at the same time that it's up to me to fix King. How do you go about fixing a person? How do you fix them without taking them apart first?

That night, King and I are sitting on the front step of the trailer eating fried chicken right out of the bucket. That's how we like it, no plates. The sun is in that perfect place in the sky where you can still see it all but you know that soon the colours will start and it will be cool enough for sleeping and breathing deep again. We're quiet, eating and waiting for that first chip to be taken from the full-circle sun.

'You think I should buy some new clothes for this week, Hazel?'

I pull the moist towelette out if its wrapper and suspect they are getting smaller. I wipe my hands slowly and dig under my nails to get all the grease. 'You know, King, I don't think I'm going to buy flypaper anymore.'

'Okay, Hazel, I never really liked that stuff anyway.'

We look at the sun a bit more, and King says, 'You know, I don't think I'll buy new clothes after all.'

'I think you're fine just how you are. Besides, you always look kind of weird in new stuff.'

He laughs. 'I know. New isn't really my style.'

We don't say anything for a while, just sit and eat chicken. And then I get tired of not saying all the things that we are thinking and I talk just to fill in the silence. 'Sure was a beautiful day today, wasn't it?'

'Nothing bad in the world today.'

'Nope,' I say, 'nothing bad in the world.'

We are quiet for a long time.

I know that everything is going to work out sooner or later. After all, I have a knack for getting myself set up. I am the proud owner of a trailer and I have King and a bunch of friends and fun times to show for myself. But sometimes, in the quiet, some old part of me wonders if I didn't just fall into this life.

My dad has this saying that he got from his dad. He would finish reading the local paper and say, 'I see that Suzie Zack and Joseph Bingle got married. Good thing for Joseph because he was just smart enough to get into a load of trouble with that girl but not smart enough to see his way to the other side.'

Here my dad would give me a glance, not a straight-in-the-eye look because he never looked me straight in the eye, but there was enough of a pause in the story and enough of a head nod in my direction to let me know that I should never get myself into any load of trouble, especially with someone not smart enough to see the other side.

He would continue. 'Good for that pair that Suzie's father owns enough of the rendering plant to make Joseph a lead hand and send him on his way.'

And here it is, here's the saying that was important enough to be passed down from his father: 'That lad fell ass backwards into his life.'

Falling ass backwards means that whoever my dad or my dad's dad was talking about didn't have a plan. He was just bumbling along letting life take him wherever it wanted, and then all of a sudden – *bang* – there he was, falling ass backwards into something.

In my dad's eyes, life is perilous: if you don't watch yourself at every turn you could end up falling ass backwards into something, and there's no telling if that something will be good, bad or worse than bad. Chance itself is frightening in my dad's world. You never want to take a step if you don't know where it will lead. And as for falling – well, that's pure foolishness.

I can hear my dad right now, sitting at some dinner table somewhere surrounded by nodding and eyebrow-lifting men just like him: 'We don't know what got into that girl. One moment she was here, safe at home, choosing a college, and the next she was living in a trailer park with some sort of lawbreaker and working at a second-hand store.'

The next part is where I fall ass backwards into something and I have no idea what that something could be.

King is going to court because he got arrested for repeated offences of disturbing the peace and trespassing and sometimes even breaking and entering. Now, getting arrested is definitely something you fall into, but all that law-breaking, well, that's something that you have to work towards. You don't build a police record by accident.

And then I take a good look at King sitting on the front step peering suspiciously at his moist towelette, and I can see him falling into some piece of unknown chance – totally comfortable. Not ass backwards but full speed ahead, with both eyes open and a crooked grin on his face. Beautiful. King's very existence would terrify my dad and my dad's dad and a hundred dads before them.

King knows something that can never be understood by people like my dad: falling is not always ass backwards. Falling itself can be a way of life.

The court thing didn't go so well.

There are so many things I don't feel like talking about. Not the new me who is Hazel, and not the old me either. Sometimes it's better to leave a gap when things get too rough, like now, or just aren't fun anymore. So you see over them to the next thing, to the next time when everything will be better and smooth. Just let them pass. Just pass the time until King comes home and is back where he belongs. This is one chunk of time that I would love to lose: I wish I could start a thought or a memory and wake up fourteen days from now and everything would be okay. But that isn't happening – I'm here and there's nothing much I can do about it except to not think at all.

In these don't-think-about-anything times, I like to be up high – not so I can jump or anything like that, but to see from a different perspective what is really just the same old thing.

There's this building in town with a fire escape that leads up to the roof. I found it on one of my walks when I first got to town. That's where I am now, around back. I grab the fire-escape ladder and climb the rusty old rungs to the roof. The building is a bingo hall, and when you're on the roof you have to be careful how you step because people can hear. There is a crowd there now: B4, O74.

I walk like a cat burglar over the bingo game and think of all the people down there who only want one thing in the world: a simple number like G57, which means a new TV.

At the end of the bingo roof, there's a gap where you could fall a storey down, but it's not too far to the next roof, where you can get to an even higher building. I jump.

This building looks like it used to be a boarding house, but now there are no people, just a lot of abandoned windows, some broken, with stained curtains blowing through the rough holes. This empty place is easy to climb, just straight up the fire escapes. I go all the way to the top. There is nothing I want to see on the inside of this place. All I want is to be on top of its five storeys, with all those empty rooms below me – five storeys is the highest building in town.

My hands smell like rust and metal from the climbing. I can see everything from here. The town is a jumble of quarry limestone, scattered from one side to the other. Entire streets of houses came piece by piece from that giant hole.

I can see right to the edge of the pit on one side of town to Old Joe's at the other end. Joe's has a blue neon sign hanging out front, blinking like it might be shorting out. The sign shows a martini being poured and an olive being plunked into the glass. Then the glass disappears and the pouring starts over again. The sign is a joke – no one would ever order a martini at Joe's.

The wind blows me safely backwards from the edge of the roof, away from the side and not over it. I decide that this is a sign that everything will be all right, until I walk to the other side and realize that from here it is the opposite. I breathe deeply so my lungs expand, opening new parts of themselves to get the most of this high-up fearless air. It feels like the first breath I've taken in days.

The trick to keeping a place wonderful is to keep your visits short. I hold my breath the best I can as I go down the five storeys so I can take the wind with me.

I start walking towards Old Joe's and realize that I don't want to go there, not today and not by myself. So I find a pay phone at the end of the block. The phone book is hanging by its wire cord and the pages are flapping loose in the wind. The cord makes this soft metallic sound when it hits the shelf. I listen to this for a while, the rustle of the pages and the soft hit. It sounds like a song waiting for words. I leave the door of the booth open while I dial so the sound can keep going.

'Sissy,' I say, 'did you ever realize how many words there are for jail?'

Sissy waits for a second, which is a long time for her, then she says, 'Hazel, we've been so worried about you. Where have you been? People have been calling here looking for you, and King called, and he said he could only call once, so now he's probably worried, just sitting somewhere worried because no one knows what you're up to. And you know, Hazel, it really pisses me off when you do stuff like this.'

'Sixteen,' I say, 'sixteen words, including the slang, of course.'

Sissy's getting all worked up now. 'Hazel, I think you should come home, I mean straight home.'

'Nah, I think I'll go for a float or something. I'm not ready to go home yet.'

And Sissy starts going off again about the phone calls and all the rest. I stop her. 'I got sixteen, Sissy. Why don't you see how many you can get, then I'll come home and we'll compare lists?'

She doesn't like this but says okay and I get off the phone.

It takes me an hour to walk to the quarry. I take gravel roads all the way so I can hear the crunch of the stones as I walk. When I get there, I realize that I don't want to float after all.

I go to the highest cliff and sit on the edge, looking down at what I can see of the water and then up at the sky. The night is getting good and dark now. The air is cold against my arms, giving me goosebumps.

Some amount of time goes by, but not enough to add up to fourteen days.

Then Spiney is sitting beside me. We don't say anything, just let our feet hang over the side of the quarry wall. Sometimes one of us hits at the cliff with a heel and a little piece of rock falls off. After a couple of seconds, it hits the water.

A lot of people think that just because you're with a person, you have to talk. It's like it's a rule but really it's a bullshit kind of pressure. There are so many good things about not talking. Not talking with Spiney has a quality all its own, maybe because he never learned the bullshit rule in the first place. And then I think, do you like not talking more when you once thought you should talk? Or is it better if you never knew the rule? If you never knew the rule, and not talking bullshit is just the way you are, do you appreciate yourself, or do you just never know the difference? I'm trying to think of a way to ask Spiney all these questions.

Just as I'm getting it figured out, Spiney says, 'Sixteen, Hazel?'

'So far.'

I need to know the answer to something I forget how to ask. How is everything going to be okay? And what is that part about falling being a good thing? I'm crying because I need to figure this out, and I need King to figure it out with me.

Spiney has his arm around me, and my nose is running. I'm getting tears on the shoulder of his T-shirt, and I'm so sure that he doesn't mind me being a mess that it makes me cry harder. I cry until all the air is out of my lungs, and I'm down to the bit of wind that I saved from the rooftop. But that goes too.

I sit up and open my eyes. The tears blur everything together: the water, the sky, the rooftop, the telephone-book noise, the gravel, the feeling of not talking to Spiney and the questions that I thought I had figured out. And then I breathe.

cage
cooler
big house
solitary
clink
detention
pen
freezer
inside
away
joint
brig
prison
slammer
lock-up
tank

I'm lying in bed alone. It's not the same night, and I don't think it's the next night either – one further down. The Newfoundland flowers are outside, and the Christmas lights are on, one flashing. The colours come through the window all mixed together: blue on the ceiling, green on the sheets and a blue crossed with a red above my belly button. I want King's hands to fall right there, to trace the cross, to erase everything and make me good.

Once King called me his nymphomaniac. 'I could tell you a story,' I said, 'but you should just know and not ask about it and not call me that again.'

He leaned back, not touching anywhere, and said, 'Why don't you tell me the story? Once upon a time there was a girl,' he started. I finished the rest in my head, just for me.

Once upon a time there was a girl without my name and she wanted something real without knowing what real might be. So she invented it from movies, from the songs in her mind and the things she read and wanted to believe. She settled for anything that felt close: love scenes, the Rolling Stones and the back seat of anything with loud music playing.

The back seat of some old car that shouldn't even be running anymore, with her foot, sock still on, against a window, and her head beside the ashtray in an armrest. A burnt dusty smell of old cigarettes. The interior light turned the holes in the vinyl roof into stars and this was love. And then she was alone in the back while somebody said, 'I gotta piss,' and the door opened and her foot fell away from the window and landed outside on the gravel. She heard swearing as someone stumbled into the ditch. The car door closed around her leg and made pinching bruises that stayed. It wasn't love, but it was real.

I could never tell this story to King. Not this story and not any of the sequels – second verse same as the first. How can you say love in the negative: un, in, im? Instead, I just put my hand on his belly and moved it up to his heart. Everything has an engine that can be fixed.

King touched me with just the tip of a fingernail, and I felt it. I wondered how in all those cars there was no feeling except a foot on a window and a head against an ashtray. And when King ran his fingernail so softly, it was everything.

King said, 'It's okay.'

And I said, 'There is no story, nothing at all.'

I think of all those years that didn't have me in them and I didn't know anything was missing. And I think about how King gave it all back to me.

The colours of the Christmas lights mix and move around the room as though the trailer is spinning. I find the floor with my foot and lie across the bed. I put the ashtray beside my head. I raise my other foot against the wall. I can smell the ashes stirring beside me.

Nothing. And nothing. I think of how easy all the hard things have become. I think of all the things that I have now, for the first time. The easiness becomes an idea that I can crawl inside. And I go.

I'm back at the thrift, and the dancers that I put in the front window so long ago seem silly today. They are still there spinning around, but it's not dancing anymore – it's more like twisting in the wind.

So I take them down and put the jewellery and the dresses and all the rest of the stuff away in the back. Now they're just leftovers, that one guy who stays too late at every party.

I go through the racks and pull out polo shirts and chinos. I pin the pants and shirts to a piece of tartan, hang it in the shop window and sit back. Half an hour later three of the six things that I pinned up are sold.

Egg is at the door. 'Hey, Hazel.'

'Hey.'

'You doing something with the window?'

'Yeah, letting it rot.'

Egg looks surprised and then drags the chairs from the back and sits down. He gets comfortable. 'I'm a good listener.'

I sit in the chair he brought for me. I don't know if I really feel like talking, but Egg has come for a visit so I start. 'I don't know. I'm just blue. Isn't a person allowed to be blue around here?'

'You just don't strike me as that kind. The kind to get blue, I mean.'

'Okay, Freud.'

I get up to put on water and Egg keeps looking at me with this expression that says, *Is everything all right?* And I keep nodding like *Everything is all right, Egg*. Even though we haven't said anything out loud, the sentiment is there and it feels kind.

'No, really,' he says when I bring back the mugs. 'Why the long face today?'

'Ahhh, nothing.' I lean back on the chair. The sun is shining through the window and it falls across my shoulders, warm and comfortable. 'Well,' I say. 'Well … '

'Your boyfriend's in jail.'

I give him a look.

'Everyone knows,' he says. 'Sorry, but they do. Sorry.'

'Yeah, I guess they would. Well, you're right. He is in jail.'

'Women like bad guys.'

'I guess they do, but there's bad guys and then there's bad guys, if you know what I mean.'

'No, not really.'

'Me neither.'

It turns out that Egg has never had a girlfriend. Not the serious kind. He chalks it up to it his belief that women like bad guys and he definitely isn't bad. Not even a little bit bad. I try to tell him that it's really not so cut-and-dry but he doesn't believe me and I guess I don't really believe me either.

Now that Egg has brought up the whole incarceration thing I feel better. I didn't know it, but I feel like I've been carrying around this big shameful secret. I feel even better when I realize that this is a small-town piece of gossip. It's one of those things that everybody in the town knows but that's it. Small-town as in only one town, not even the next town over, and definitely not the town where my parents live.

So we sit and talk. The funny thing is that people come into the shop and linger around where we're sitting – they eavesdrop while going through the racks. Egg and I talk about the bad guy–good guy thing for a while. And then we talk about how a relationship is always lopsided, how one partner is the lover and the other one is the loved, and then we talk about which one we would rather be.

Sometimes people join in. One man sits and chats for a while about how he just retired and is trying to figure out what to do with his time. A woman calls across the shop that the lopsided relationship can change sides in an instant – you never get to be one or the other forever. The eavesdropping seems to make people stay in the shop long enough to dig through the heaps of stuff and find something that they want.

It turns out that there's quite a pile of cash by the time we close up. Egg and I count the till and figure out that the shop made more money today than over the past two weeks put together.

'Not bad at all,' I say to Egg.

He grins. 'Same time tomorrow?'

'Don't you have anything to do?'

'Nope,' he says and grins like he's proud of the fact.

'Well then, it's a date.'

Egg gives me one of his shy looks and takes off down the street.

All the talking took the edge off the day. But now it's home time and I'm not looking forward to that at all. Plus I'm kind of pissed that Egg is right. People all over town know that King is in the pen and I'm already hating them for looking at me and thinking, 'Hey, that's the girl who's going out with that guy in jail.' And really, what the hell is so bad about King being in jail anyway?

Maybe the greatest thing about living with King in the park is the honesty. There's no pretending that you're perfect and that you always sit up straight, even when no one is around. You can just be your own slouchy self if you want. No questions, no judgments.

I remember my mom giving me some advice before one of her parties: 'Pretend that there is a big movie camera right over your shoulder and that everything you do is being filmed for all the world to see.'

So I did the movie-camera thing. I did it until the guests left the house and then for the rest of the day. I did the camera thing all that week and the next. And she was right: it worked, it made me a better person. I was always on guard against un-movie-like behaviour, and in my parents' house that meant fewer raised eyebrows and more money. The camera was my ticket to ride.

'Forget it,' I say out loud when I get into the Duster. Tomorrow I will wear black-and-white stripes. I will work at the shop, I will talk to Egg, I will have a bit of fun. For now I'll just drive around until I'm tired and then I'll go back to the park and crash out.

Nine days left.

There's this great song by the Tragically Hip with a line that goes 'When it starts to fall apart, man, it really falls apart.' That's what I'm singing in my head as I drive the Duster to the pen.

I decided to call it the pen. The name reminds me of the place where Sissy keeps Buck the chicken, and I have to say that she sure does take good care of that thing. So I'm on my way to the pen singing the 'when it starts to fall apart' song and thinking of the road ahead.

I'm almost there. I decide to change my song and try to think up something more positive. Something with the words 'come together' and not 'fall apart,' but all I can think of is that John Lennon song that I don't like, so I'm stuck with the original as I pull into the parking lot of the c-o-r-r-e-c-t-i-o-n-a-l f-a-c-i-l-i-t-y.

The pen.

Park. Get out. Walk. Smile.

I'm admitted by a guy who looks mean, and led to a room by a guy who looks meaner.

I put on my favourite dress for this occasion. It's full of flowers and glamour. When I look down at the fabric, something makes me think of France. I've never seen the place, but somehow this is France. I applied all the liquid eyeliner I could find a spot for on my eyelids, and my lips are full of red, Russian red to be exact. Finally, the song I'm playing in my head has changed to 'Lara's Theme.' Dump trucks, when they're backing up, play the first notes of this song – da da da da da da da da dum da. A semi-tone. There's so much beauty in the world, it's just that most people don't know where to look.

The ceilings here are impossibly high. It's like this place was built to march a tribe of giants through. The visiting room looks like a school lunchroom, but the people sitting around sure don't look like anybody I ever went to school with. The table I'm sitting at looks like the kind of place where people can talk and visit without really being together. I start to understand what 'institutional' means. Good thing I painted my toenails this morning.

Then there's King dressed in blue. That's his colour. He sits in the chair opposite me and reaches his hand across the table. His hand is clean, no grease under the fingernails. His palms have never been soft before – usually they're calloused and dirty. King looks older and younger at the same time. He looks like he's getting a lot of sleep. He looks like he's still sleeping.

'You know, King, there's this kind of crab – it's called a giant crab. If you measure it from claw to claw, it's six feet.'

He looks up at me and then takes a breath like he's going to say something, but then he doesn't. I wait. He takes another breath and says, 'You know, Hazel, there's this kind of fish that lives on the bottom of the ocean, a flounder, and when it's born it has eyes on opposite sides of its head, but as it gets older one of its eyes moves so it can be beside the other.'

'How does that happen?'

'I don't know. It's just one of those freak growing, evolution things. I think it swims on its side.'

'What's my real name?' I say.

'Hazel,' he says. And I smile and feel a little bit of the last days lifting off my shoulders.

'Do you like my dress?'

'No, I love your dress.'

And we sit for a while, waiting for nothing.

Then he says, 'You know what's the worst? The echoes. The echoes are the worst. One little noise and I swear you can hear it for hours.'

I look around the room, like there still might be an echo flying around somewhere close.

I say, 'Sometimes when you're sleeping, I listen to you breathe, and in the spaces, I can hear the words "I love you" over and over.'

And he smiles with all the sleep wiped off his face, and he holds my hand tighter. 'You know,' I say, 'maybe this whole thing is just one of those freak growing, evolution things. Maybe this is just us growing and evolving. Things can only get better from here.'

We make funny faces at each other until it's time to go.

When we stand, our shoulders are back, our chins are up. King gives me a grin and says, 'You take care of you.'

I nod and shrug like *Of course I will*, then give him a big grin right back and turn away.

Now when I walk down the corridor it seems as if the ceilings aren't tall enough, like there's not enough room in this whole building for me when I've had a good dose of King.

I drive home, and a new song comes into my head. It's happy and promising, with full orchestration. I put all the pieces together: violins, drums, bass, guitar and even a French horn. I keep the music together. Swell and fade, swell and fade. It's just starting to get to the good bit, and then it falls apart. It's hard to juggle all those instruments. It's especially hard when you're making it up as you go along.

King's home.

We go out to Old Joe's, Sissy and Spiney and King and I. The night is going fine even though there's no caps and no line dancing or anything crazy. The silent rule of the night is to not talk about the pen.

So we talk about old things, the things that brought us together. We tell the kind of stories that you might repeat to strangers. Old Joe is doing his best to make us feel like everything is normal, like we can just walk in there and tear it up like we do. He keeps bringing the beers like always and never lets us down with the bill.

The strange thing is that I find myself looking at Joe to make sure things are okay. It's like he's my reference point, my touchstone. I keep looking at him all night, and every time I look at him, he's looking right back at me like he's waiting for the answer to some question he asked a long time ago.

Sissy, for once, is talking on just one topic, telling stories in that never-ending way she has. She's a good storyteller – she can remember everything down to the smallest detail, like how there was a strange guy sitting in the bar on one particular night who kept shouting out trivia answers to questions that nobody asked, or how we found a skateboard with only three wheels and spent the rest of the night looking for the missing one.

Now she's telling about the night that King and I stole a bulldozer from the construction site and drove it to Sissy and Spiney's trailer to give them a ride into town. I had forgotten about that.

But here it is in full before me. How King was at the controls of the dozer, and I was sitting on the motor, and we were yelling to one another over the noise. It was cool and wonderful and we knew at the time that we were being totally us and in love. But here we are with this story being told like some sort of long-ago myth. At the time, I thought it was just one crazy night in a long string of crazy nights. But the crazy nights haven't been coming around much anymore.

Sissy starts the story of how King and I first hooked up but I can't listen, so I go to get us another pitcher. When I get back, King is also remembering, but mostly he's remembering the days before me, which makes sense if you want to be logical about it – I haven't been around all that long. King talks about when he was in the band with Spiney and doing all sorts of things that I wasn't around for, taking mushrooms and jamming, getting into loads of trouble, ending up lost somewhere hours away from home. He's remembering being crazy without a care in the world. Spiney and King are having a great time. The thing for me is that I think memories are great and all, but they're over.

New things all the time, that's my motto. But on this night, I feel like I'm in this strange type of purgatory where there are only repeats. Some of the stories seem familiar, and other stories happened so long ago that they shouldn't even count anymore. But the stories without me in them are completely foreign. I don't even recognize King when Spiney says, 'Remember that gig up north and the rider was all you could drink?'

And then King lists off a whole bunch of people that I have never heard of. Guys with names like Dopey and Sandman, and everybody laughs about how those guys weren't even in the band but they drank the rider all night anyway. I don't even know what a rider is.

I sit and listen to the stories and I hear Spiney say, 'Those were the days.'

King says, 'It was the best of times, it was the best of times.' Sissy, Spiney and King all laugh.

The whole night takes place in the past tense. Finally I've had enough and I figure that if I know King he has had enough of this too, so I look at him and say, 'Hey, let's go do something that we've never done.'

He looks at me like I'm proposing the strangest thing and lets the comment fall flat. No one picks it up. So we drink more beer and at the end of the night we just go home to the trailer.

We don't do the normal thing of having a couple more beers after the bar, just being together and talking down the night. This night, we get ready for bed in an orderly fashion, even brushing and flossing. It's quiet and we go to bed. The lights are off, even the Christmas lights. It is totally dark inside the trailer – not even the moon is coming in.

Today I was so excited about the homecoming that I cleaned the trailer, so everything smells good and fresh. The sheets are laundered and made up so that when we get into bed there is the smell of detergent.

We pull back the sheets and climb in, letting the covers settle around us, waiting for everything to warm up. But there is no touching, nothing. The bed gets warm as we just lie there. I don't know how to begin touching him. Then King says my name.

'Hazel?'

'Yeah.'

'This is nice.'

'I missed you.'

But saying it out loud feels strange all of a sudden. And then, just like that, we fall asleep. I guess it's all the beer and the warm bed.

We're sitting around in the trailer. We're not really saying anything, but after all the talking last night about things that happened when I wasn't around I feel like I'm missing parts of the story – big parts.

'You never talk about growing up,' I say. I'm trying to sound casual like I'm just making conversation.

'Nope.'

'Why?'

'I hate thinking about it, you know that.'

'Because you hate your parents, I know, but why?'

'You haven't met them. You don't get it.'

'Tell me then.'

'They're dumb. They don't talk.'

'What? Like deaf and dumb?'

'No, like stupid. They have nothing to say. Ever.' King makes a face. 'Stupid, boring,' he says and goes all bucktooth cross-eyed.

'They can't be that bad.'

'Oh yeah?'

'You turned out okay.'

'Fuck, Hazel, I'm not. Look at me, paralyzed – I can't do a thing.'

'Yeah, poor you. Everybody thinks you're great.'

'Everybody is a moron.'

'Thanks a lot.'

I look at him, waiting for an apology, but he doesn't say anything. He just sits for a while digging at the dirt under his nails. Finally he looks up and sees me still staring at him. 'Just drop it, okay? Back off. You start asking questions and I'm supposed to talk about things I don't want to talk about. Just let me not think for once.'

He gets up and looks in the fridge for a beer. I know we don't have any but I don't tell him, I let him root around.

'What did they do?' I say. 'Lock you in a shed or something?'

'If they did they would think it was funny.'

King slams the fridge door and the stuff on top rattles. The salt shaker crashes to the floor and salt spills all over the place.

Here's something I never told anyone. And King's never told anyone either – officially.

When we started dating, we spent all our time together. King would come straight to the trailer after work and stay all night. I never asked if he was going to come back the next day or the one after that. He just did.

One night we were out celebrating because we had decided that King was going to move into Even More for real. We were too excited to stay in the little trailer so we headed out. Sissy and Spiney came too but they couldn't keep up, so they went home and King and I hung around and talked and drank and talked.

I don't think I have ever known someone as well as I know King. Lots of talking with complete understanding. We talked about everything that happened in our lives, things that we wished would happen and things that we were going to make happen hell or high water. Every time we said something sad the sadness was a little easier to take and when we shared a happy story it was all the better. King would say, 'Here it comes, Hazel. Buckle up!' When we realized that we were just sitting and smiling at one another we decided to beat it out of there. Old Joe kept shaking his head and grinning when we said good night.

By the time we left we were pretty loady. We were leaning on one another as we walked down the street. I was thinking out loud, 'Left, right and again,' so that I could get my feet to move in order. King kept stopping and picking me up and swirling me around, saying, 'Abracadabra, open sesame, shazam!'

We headed down the side roads out of town. The night was gorgeous and clear. King and I kept right on talking through the whole walk. By this time I was telling him about my parents and what it was like to live with them.

When we were about halfway up the highway we decided to take a break and settle into the ditch. We lay back and talked about constellations for a while and then, right out of what I thought was nowhere, King started a story.

'Hazel, my parents are farmers.'

'Yeah, you told me.'

'I hated growing up on their farm. Another farm coulda been cool, but their farm was hell.'

'Okay,' I said. I waited while King took a breath and pointed out Orion.

'One day when I was about nine I was seeding the back paddock. Do you know how you do that?'

'No.'

'When you're seeding, you carry this heavy bag of seed over your shoulder and you do this thing called broadcasting, where you take a handful of seed and you spread it around in wide arcs while you walk in a straight line. Then you turn around at the end of the field and move over and start again.'

King made a wide gesture with his arm to show the broadcasting. From where I was sitting it looked like he was throwing the stars up into the sky. Then he stopped himself, lit up a cigarette and took a drag. For a second I thought that was the end of the story.

'I finished the paddock and dragged the rest of the seed back to the barn. My dad was there mucking the horses and he took one look at me and started going off: "Do you know how much grass seed costs?" And "Goddamn you, why did you use half a bag for a couple of mangy horses?" I looked down and saw that the seed bag was half gone. More gone than it should have been.

'Then I looked behind me and I was trailing a line of grass seed. There was a hole in the bag. Must have been some mice into it. The line of seed looked funny stretching back and forth across the field and then leading right to my feet. It was like one of those Roadrunner cartoons with the powder that leads to the dynamite. And I was the coyote who just realized that I was going to blow myself up. So I never saw it coming. My dad backhanded me right across the head. That and the weight of the seed bag landed me on my ass.'

'Oh shit, King. I'm sorry,' I said and I tried to put my arm around him but he was sitting stiff as a board so I backed off. We just sat for a minute or two.

'That's not the best part.'

'Okay.'

'The next day I had a black eye. A bad one where it goes purple right away and your eye is bloodshot. It was swollen and going to get worse. My mom never said anything, she just handed me some aspirin at breakfast. And dad said that we were going into town to the co-op. Do you know what a co-op is?'

'Yeah, we had one too.'

'My dad said that I better break my piggy bank because I was buying a bag of grass seed today. So that's what I did and we went into town. When we were at the co-op, a couple of old farmers patted me on the back and said things like "I'd hate to see the other guy." Bullshit like that. I nodded at them, which hurt because my eye was swollen almost shut and it hurt even worse every time I moved. Then we were at the checkout and the clerk said, "How did you get that, boy?" My dad was right there with the bag of seed in his hand staring at me. The clerk asked again so I said something like "Walking into a door" or some damn stupid thing like that. But the clerk wouldn't let it go. He kept asking, "Now tell me, how did you get it?" All I could see was my boots and my dad's white knuckles holding the seed.

'I didn't say anything but no one was moving so I started, "I was out in the back paddock and I was seeding."

'My dad put the bag down and hovered over me. "Go on, son," he said, "tell them." I couldn't look him in the eye so I just nodded and stared at the floor. I said the first thing I could think of. "I was in the back paddock seeding and walked backwards into the electric fence and got shocked."

'"That doesn't give you no black eye, son," the clerk said.

'So I went on. "Then I snagged the loop of my pants on a nail in the post."

'The clerk and my dad started laughing so I kept going. "I tried to push myself off the post but I kept getting shocked. So I started kicking to get my pants unhitched and I kicked so hard that I went headfirst into the mud."

'The clerk and my dad were howling now and other people were coming around to see what all the fuss was about. "I must have landed on a rock," I said.

'My dad kept slapping his leg and saying he wished he was there to see me dangling on that fence, and he paid for the grass seed without even looking at me. The people who had come over because of the laughing wanted to hear the story so my dad said, "Tell them, son. Tell them how you got that shiner."

'So I repeated the story and got more slaps on the back and everyone thought the kid with the black eye was pretty great.

'That day my dad took me to the hardware store and to the diner. All over the damned town so he could let his friends in on the joke.

'By the time we got home I was right screwed. My eye was even more swollen and I had a killer headache. My eyelid was about to burst open because there was too much swelling and blood. It needed to be cut so that the pressure could be let off. You know, like when a fighter gets a black eye in the ring and the trainer cuts it open a bit. But I didn't have a chance to do anything about it all day. By the time I got out of the truck I thought I was going to throw up, either that or pass out. But I didn't, and my dad came around to my side and put his hand on my shoulder and said, "I'm real proud of you, son."'

We were quiet for a moment. I couldn't think of anything to say. 'Holy shit, King.'

'Yeah.'

'Man.'

'Hazel?'

'Yeah?'

'That was just a day. You know? Just one.'

'King, you're out now.'

'Yeah,' he said and took a deep breath. 'But the rest of this mess is all me.' He patted himself proudly on the chest. 'I did the rest myself.'

And then leaned over and whispered into my ear. 'It's like you came along and cut my eye,' he said and looked at me. I could see him clearly, for a moment, as a little kid with a black eye. Then he leaned back for a big belly laugh. 'Not very romantic, is it?' He laughed again. 'But really, thanks.'

We lay in the ditch for a long time and I guess we passed out because next thing I knew the sun was coming up and we were all dusty.

We walked the rest of the way back to the park and immediately crashed out again. Then we woke up and after a bunch of glasses of water King said to me, 'How did we get home last night?'

'What do you mean?'

'I don't remember getting home at all.'

'Really?'

'Yeah. I remember paying the bill, but that's about it.'

'Oh.'

I looked at him for a while and realized that he wasn't looking back at me. Not right into my eyes anyway. And then he turned around and started going through the fridge. 'Hangover munchies,' he said.

'We just walked,' I said, 'along the highway.'

'Anything exciting?'

'You don't remember?'

He turned around and stared at me like he was daring me. We were frozen like that for a second.

'No,' he said again, 'I don't remember a thing.'

'Me neither. Not really,' I said.

So now I'm looking at the salt that was spilled on the floor wondering what we're pretending to forget now.

I saw these two kids in the supermarket one time, a big sister and her younger brother. The brother was being a brat, dumping boxes off shelves and grabbing things from his sister. And then the sister had enough of it so she went over and hugged him. Not hard, and she didn't secretly pinch him or anything, but I saw her expression behind his back and her eyes were closed tight and she was gritting her teeth. She was giving a bad hug. The little boy started crying and the mom rushed over and said, 'What the hell is going on here?'

And the girl shrugged her shoulders and looked all innocent and said, 'I just hugged him.'

I got a bad hug today. King was getting ready to go to work and I was watering the wildflowers. Before he got on his bike I threw down the water gun, ran over to him and said, 'Come on, give it up.'

He just looked at me and slowly put on his motorcycle helmet. I stood there half waiting for him to fasten his helmet and half not believing that he wasn't hugging me. Once he had his helmet on, face shield down, he leaned in and gave me a hug.

What that little girl knew and what her brother knew and what I know is that a hug can be a weapon. It can even be the opposite of an *I love you*, it can be an *I don't care*.

I ran over to where he was getting on the bike and gave him a shove. 'Talk to me!'

King turned his head towards me but I couldn't see his expression through the helmet shield. His voice came muffled. 'Don't, Hazel. Please.'

The jamming has started and King's gone a lot. After that long night of reminiscing at the bar, King and Spiney got some of the guys from the old band together and rented a trailer at the far end of the park so that they can go and jam whenever they want. The first problem about the whole set-up is that they had some complaints because their music was too loud, so they had to move the trailer even further away. Now it's a twenty-minute walk from home.

The second problem is that there's a bit of a swamp on that side of the park. The earth feels solid, but just underneath the surface is mud. The mud is the whole reason the park stops where it does. Only they didn't know about the swamp when they moved the trailer. After jamming almost every night, the vibrations from the music have sort of settled the rig. The jacks have been swallowed up by the swamp, and now the trailer's just kind of keeping itself up, jiggling away on top of the mud. But they figure that it doesn't really matter.

At night, when King is gone, I go over and visit Sissy and we keep each other company. Sometimes they're gone until really late, and Sissy and I sit in her trailer and talk. Well, we talk as much as anyone can talk to Sissy, meaning that I listen to her until really late. But that's okay too. Sissy and I haven't really had a ton of time to hang out just the two of us.

Tonight is the sixth night in a row that the boys have jammed. It's getting really late now. I didn't feel like listening to Sissy again so I just stayed home. I'm trying to remember all the things I did before I knew King. I'm also drinking a big bottle of JD. I think of going over to Old Joe's and hanging out for a while and talking to him while he's behind the bar. I used to do that a lot.

But Sissy and I went there the other night and some people asked us if it was true that the old band was getting back together. I thought, Why don't you ask them yourselves? But then Sissy told them that we didn't know what was going on. I didn't like that because it made things seem out of control. It made me feel like a stranger in King's life.

King used to come home from the motorcycle shop and tell me about all the things he was fixing and about problems he was having with getting the right parts and stuff like that. Now I feel like I'm just a girlfriend. I've never been *the girlfriend* in my whole new Hazel life.

It's three-thirty.

I try to sleep for a while, but the more I'm alone the more I get pissed off that I'm alone. I'm lying on the bed with my clothes still on, and I don't feel tired at all. As a matter of fact, I feel more awake than I do in the day. It's funny how the night can do that to you, how in those stolen hours while everyone else is stopped and sleeping, your life is still progressing.

And then I know the answer, the answer that I've known all night, and I give in to it. I really just want King here and not in that stupid sinking trailer with Spiney and two other guys that I don't really like. So I decide to take that twenty-minute walk, go and get him and say, 'Come on home now because home is where I want you and where you should be at this particular moment.' He will understand exactly what I mean because that's just the way he is.

I don't really know the other two guys from the band, so I figure that it's a good idea to look great when showing up unannounced to take King away. I put on liquid eyeliner and a great and glamorous dress that I save for special occasions. It only takes two or three minutes to get myself put together but when I look in the mirror I have to admit that I did a pretty damn good job. I put on my shoes, grab my bottle of Jack Daniel's and go for a walk.

But now that I'm on the way there, I'm wondering if maybe this is the wrong thing to do. I especially think that it's the wrong thing when I start to feel cold and I still have another fifteen minutes of walking to do. But then I think of going back to the trailer and sitting on the couch or lying awake by myself in bed, and I know that going to get King is the only thing for me to do right now.

I make my way between the trailers singing songs about life on the road. It seems to get a little warmer now that I have fully committed to my task. Things aren't so up in the air anymore either. I imagine that when I get close to the practice trailer, I'll hear the songs I've heard on the band's demo tape that King plays at home. I imagine that a song will end just as I walk into the trailer. King will see me and smile because he knows I'm wearing a special dress just for this night and he'll think I'm the best thing he's ever seen. Then he'll come over and ask if I heard the music. I'll say sure, I heard a bit, and he'll ask if I liked it. I'll say that it was great, and he'll say it's really cool that you're here so we can walk home together. Then he'll put down his bass and we'll go home and lie in bed. And we'll talk until dawn and fall asleep wrapped up in each other.

By the time I run through the scenario in my head, I'm feeling pretty good. The night air has woken me up more than before, and I'm feeling this strange and complete clarity. The park and the stars and everything I put my eyes on is absolutely beautiful and close. Even More is even more beautiful than you could ever expect from a trailer park. It's like I've never seen this stretch of road or these trailers before. The colours show their real beauty under the moon, and I'm the only one here to see the greatness of everything. It's just for me. And very, very quietly I thank the colours and the moon and the air for turning into such a beautiful silver glow in the middle of the night. Then I'm at the edge of the park, and I can see the trailer and hear the instruments.

As I get closer, I try to figure out the tune, but it's like nothing I've ever heard King play before. I definitely don't recognize it. Not from the demo tape. Not from anything. I try to listen to the bass that I know King is playing, and I can't recognize anything of him in the notes. I move closer and listen. The grass outside the trailer has never been cut, and the wetness of it makes my dress heavy and cold with dew. The bottom of the hem sticks uncomfortably around my legs so it gets hard to walk.

The music is getting much louder now, and all the light and colours of the night fade as I focus on the trailer. I step up onto the boards that the guys have laid down so they don't get stuck in the swamp. The music is really loud now, almost to the point where I don't want to get any closer. It's not good music either. I stop in the middle of the boards, not far from and not close to the front door. All the bass notes are angry and they don't match anything that anyone else is playing.

I take a swig from the bottle of JD, and I realize that the band is trying to play a song. But there's a problem, and that problem is King.

He's playing twice as fast and three times as mean as the rest of the guys. I listen as they try to keep up with him, and then one by one they give up and all that's left is King. The guys try to start up again, but the same thing happens, and they stop, and it's only King.

Now don't get me wrong – I'm all over fast and mean songs because they serve a purpose in life, a soundtrack when you're feeling fast and mean. But there is definitely something wrong here, something that I can't quite name except to say the word 'desperation' over and over in my head. This is something I've never heard, and especially something I've never heard from King. I don't want to go into the trailer, and I don't want to leave either, because suddenly I'm very worried about just about everything.

Then a big crash comes from inside and the trailer door bursts open. King is there in the doorway looking into the night with the meanest expression I've ever seen on a face. When he sees me, he goes blank. I look right back at him and then straighten my wet dress around my legs. When I look back up he's still staring at me, but now he has an expression on his face that I can't read.

Behind King I can see the inside of the trailer, the guys, the amps and cords and wires lying all over, and someone sitting on the floor. A girl. A girl that I don't want to remember.

I want to tell King something, but I can't think. So I slowly lean down and set the bottle of JD on the boards and turn and walk away.

I'm watching where I step as I wade through the grass, holding up my skirt so that it doesn't twist around my legs and trip me up. I make my way back to the limits of the park, where the grass is cut. I feel myself getting further from the sinking trailer with every step. I walk home slowly. All I can think of is the expression on King's face, and how it didn't belong there. And how that wasn't the only thing that didn't belong in the trailer. I try to think of how much I had to drink tonight. Not enough to hallucinate.

Then I hear noises behind me. I know without looking that King is following me home. I can hear his drunken walk and the clink of the bottle as it hits his teeth when he takes a drink. But I can't look back. I slow down a little and then he is beside me.

We don't say a thing while we're walking to the trailer. I keep looking down, still holding my dress with the wet hem. I can see the tips of King's shoes keeping step with the tips of mine.

This lasts a long time.

When we get to our front lawn, he stops behind me and reaches out. I can feel the ends of his fingers just touch my shoulder before he lets his arm fall. I stop and let go of my hem, still not looking up. King moves so that he is in front of me. I can feel him close so that the small space between our bodies warms up a little. He drops the bottle and puts his hands on either side of my face. He tilts my head up so that we are facing one another. At first I can't look him in the eyes, but I can tell he is waiting and he won't stop, so I look.

Then I can see that he is crying. There is no expression on his face. We stare at one another for a while, then he hugs me, pulls me really close and hugs me like he's trying to squeeze our bodies so tight together that they will become one thing. At first I don't want to touch him at all. At first I want to yell and scream and push. But I can feel him shaking. I move and hug him back. He lets out a big breath like he's been holding something in for a long time and leans down so that we can be even closer. I can hear him crying into my shoulder, and I hold him as tightly as he is holding me.

'It's going to be okay,' I whisper. 'Everything's good.'

I can feel him nod his head against my neck.

'Everything's good.'

It's been almost a week now since the last jam. The guys from the band have been calling and asking when King is going to come out again. I overhear him say that he's really tired and maybe coming down with something. He's lying – he's feeling fine. But there is something going around, at least in our trailer.

King walks with his head down and, sometimes, shuffles his feet. There is something missing from a place that used to be full. The missing thing is that sparkle that makes you get out of bed at four-thirty on a beautiful night and go outside just to smell the air. The missing thing isn't just in King – it's in me too. When you love someone, and their night-air-smelling tendencies go out the window, yours do too.

The other night, I tried asking King what was wrong, like did something happen in jail. He said no, that it was something else, but he hasn't figured out what. He said that some extra gravity is weighing on him. And that's about the most we've talked since the jam breakdown. Things have been quiet, as if even talking about the weather would lead to a big blow-up.

I went back to my old motto – action not words. It's Friday night, and I know from unintentional eavesdropping that King is staying home this weekend. So, I figure, why not have a back-to-basics session: get done with all this crap and ease the talk, big or small, with general drunkenness. So all of this leads me to where I am now, and that is trudging home with a whole lot of booze. Booze is basically a bad thing when you see the medical stats and side effects of long-term use, but it can cure almost every communication problem on a short-term basis. I got vodka and Clamato for Caesars and spiced rum and Coke for a little craziness, and a six-pack for the in-between times.

I wouldn't even mind a fight right now, a real good yelling one, just to get things started. Any kind of talking would be good at this point. That's what the spiced rum is for: every time King drinks it, he starts talking and just never shuts up. So I got a forty for good measure.

Despite the heaviness of the booze bags, I'm feeling pretty great about the day. It's hot but not the kind of hot where you can't do a thing without breaking a sweat. It's hot in the way that makes huge amounts of dust fly up off the road every time a car goes past – the kind of hot that makes the world into a spaghetti western. From here I can see the heat shimmering right across the whole park. It makes the place look like it's under water.

As I come up to the trailer, I can see King sitting on the front step. Heat waves shimmer at his feet, and he seems so still that he could be one of those petrified animals in a museum of natural history. He's silent but I can tell that there's a whole lot going on underneath the surface.

I walk over and give him a shove. He looks up and moves to shove back, but I dodge and laugh and run up the stairs. He gets up, and I watch him unwind from himself like I'm seeing the whole museum stir and come alive right before my eyes. He follows me into the trailer to see what I've got in all these bags. I can hear his feet on the floor behind me – they're not dragging, and I take this as a good sign.

I hold up the bottle and say, 'Treats.'

He grins and says, 'Oh god, Hazel, you have a plan.' He rolls his eyes, but I can tell he's amused because he's grinning and looking through the rest of the bags. He holds up the bottle of vodka and the Clamato and says, 'The drink of Kings.'

And now it's time for me to laugh. It feels so good that I stretch it out. 'Hey, funny guy, where have you been?' I say. But I don't wait for the answer as I pull out the beer. 'Why don't we start on the front steps?'

'Better yet,' he grins that lopsided grin that always gets me, 'let's go for a hike.'

Things are turning out better than I expected. I love a drunken hike, especially on a day like this. We put all the gear and some extra clothes and towels into a backpack and take the long way out of the park towards the quarry. We're singing bits of songs that we like. I start the chorus and he finishes with some funny twist, mostly silly dirty lyrics. It's a game we used to play all the time.

I'm not leading the way, and I don't think King is either – we just walk and drink our beers and every now and then we say something like 'Look at that' and point to a cool wildflower or a piece of bark that looks like a face.

We're in the last truly hot part of the day, when the sun is still fierce in the sky, but in an hour or so you will be able to look up and see it deciding to head to the horizon.

We get to the quarry, strip down and jump in. The water is the coldest thing around. I can feel the dust from the road streaming off me every time I move. I put my head under and come up again, getting ready for a float. King has swum out to the middle of the quarry and is looking at me and treading water. He's pretty far away – I can see his head and shoulders but not the expression on his face. Then he says, 'Hazel, you look great.'

It sounds strange coming from so far across the water.

The neat thing about swimming in the quarry is that no matter how far away you are from the other person, you can practically whisper and the words float right across the surface of the water. King is far on the other side right now, but I can hear him speak like his lips are right at my ear.

'Thanks,' I say back after a while.

It's weird to see King as he is right now, just his head sticking above the water in a circle of small ripples. I watch one slide along the surface. It comes towards me and breaks against my chest.

I swim out to where he is. 'What do you want to do now?' I say. 'Want to race?'

'Nah,' he says.

'Float?'

'No.'

'Anything?'

'Not really,' he says.

'King?'

'Yeah.'

'I think I need a change.'

'Like what?'

'I don't know, maybe taking some kind of lessons.'

'That's cool.'

'What do you need?' I say.

He doesn't say anything, and I float for a while. Finally, 'Damned if I know.'

'Well, it's weird.'

'Hazel, look, it's just the same.'

'No, it's not.'

'Aw, hell, can we just drop all this crap?'

'Okay, let's drop it,' I say. And then after a second, 'King?'

'Yeah?'

'You ever wonder what you're doing? Like what's after this?'

'Nope.' He arches his eyebrows and starts swimming towards the shore. He calls back to me, 'This is it, Hazel. This is what I'm doing. Right now I'm swimming, in one minute I'll be drinking. If you want to know what happens after that, stick around. If not, then don't.'

Scuba-diving lessons – that would do the trick.

It took me a couple of days but I finally figured it out. The trick is that King has to be in a good mood tonight if he's going to pick up on the big 'after this' idea that I worked out for him. I cook lots of fun food: fries, pigs in a blanket, tiny egg rolls. The frozen-food part of the grocery store is our favourite.

'Hey, you know what?' I speak casually like it's no big deal.

'What?'

'Today I was singing that song that you guys wrote. You know the one, it goes, "Mystery, it's such a misery, how you don't seem to be … la la la." You know that one?'

'Yeah.'

'I couldn't get it out of my head. It's really catchy.'

King starts humming. 'I like that one too. It was an easy one to write.'

'Was it?'

King has perked up a little now. He sits back from the table and smiles. 'We just started jamming and then Scotty started to sing along and we had a song.'

'That sounds pretty magical.'

'The easiest ones are the best.'

'You haven't jammed in a long time,' I say. I take a drink and look at him out of the corner of my eye, gauging his mood. 'More fries or anything?'

'No thanks,' says King. He's sitting back and grinning now.

'So why not?'

'I'm full.'

'No, I mean why haven't you jammed? I would love to hear that song live. I only ever heard you do it acoustically and then there's that version on the demo that you guys did. But, you know, live would be cool.'

'Well, you could come out to the trailer.'

'Oh yeah?' I open us a couple of beers. 'I bet Sissy would like to come out too, you know, to see Spiney and all that.'

'I hate it when too many people are crammed in there.'

I have a quick flash of the caps girl crowded into the trailer but I don't mention it. Instead I say, 'Yeah, the trailer is pretty small.'

'I wish we could have a party in there but it won't work,' he says. He takes a drink and then swirls the beer around in the bottle.

I start singing again, 'It's such a mystery ... '

A grin starts at the corners of his mouth. 'You know, maybe we could have a party. We have a new version of that song and it rocks, I mean it *rawks*,' he says and holds up his fingers to make the rock 'n' roll sign.

'You used to play at Old Joe's, didn't you?'

'Yeah, we used to tear up that joint.'

'I wish I could have seen you in those days.'

He picks me up and twirls me and sets me down again.

'I'm going to Spiney's,' he says, and he's out the front door like a shot, running in his bare feet, in too much of a hurry for shoes.

Sissy, Spiney, King and I are out at Old Joe's. The mood in our trailer has lifted a bit since King got his big idea to have a gig so I'm hoping to cash in on some fun.

I forgot to eat dinner before heading out to the bar and now I'm feeling kind of sick. How many times do I have to learn the eat-before-you-drink lesson? But then there's King hoisting a pint and saying, 'Liquid lunch, baby,' and here I am hoisting and laughing right along with him.

I try to walk away from the table like I'm going on just a regular old bathroom trip but I know that I'm all weavy and wobbly. I make it to the stall just in time to throw up my last pint. Glamorous.

I can't bear to look at myself in the mirror. I wanted to have fun so badly that I drank my way straight past fun and into sick without even noticing. I head for the door but turn back to the mirror right away. I have to look – what if there's beer barf in my hair? This is all too familiar and it makes me feel like throwing up all over again.

Teenage sleazebag, I say to myself as I look in the mirror. Sounds like the title of a bad drive-in movie, but it's also the title of me. Not me Hazel but me before my new life, before the Duster and before everything good came along. Back then I was two people: during the day I was perfect, honour-roll popular, but after school, if I had just the right amount of vodka, I did all the wrong things with every wrong person who happened to be around.

I splash water on my face and think about who I used to be. I throw up again and decide to hang out in the bathroom for a while. This bathroom looks like every bathroom in every dive. But right now it reminds me of the bathroom at the bar I used to go to – the Blue Horizon, the Blue Ho, the Blue; take your pick. It was the typical hotel bar you would expect to find in a small town, where no one from 'away' ever wanted to spend the night.

The real action at the Blue was at the pool table in the back room. This was my crowd. The back room crawled with dropouts and guys who went to juvie in Grade Seven and never made it to high school at all. There was a never-ending circuit of characters forever in and out of town. They did adventurous things like work on oil tankers or live at logging camps for months on end. Eventually they would get fired and end up back at the Blue with a fistful of dollars to buy rounds, millionaires for one night.

The coolest guys were the ones who pulled the greatest capers, fought the dirtiest fights and said the rudest things to the police. The downside of this was that the true legends and role models of the scene were never around. The champs were mostly in jail or on the lam.

At the Blue, sex was something that you did for fun when you weren't quite ready to go home. Some guy called Slader or Vic or Cooper or Smithy or Whoever would give me the look and say something like, 'Leaving now?'

'Yeah.'

'Need a lift?'

'Yeah.'

And that was that. We were off to the Mustang or Camaro or Chevelle or Firebird or Whatever. If you were smart you brought a traveller and drank on your way to a country road. The cool guys never minded. The really cool guys had a traveller or two themselves. Mostly I was struggling with my zipper before the car even stopped. Why waste time?

Afterwards, I would get whoever to drop me off downtown so I could walk home and sober up a little. I walked with my secrets and my wrong-side-of-town-ness all the way to my parents' house. On those walks from downtown back to the 'right' side of town I could imagine the secrets trailing behind me. I kept them close. They kept me company when I got home.

This was all going on around the time my mother gave up pretending she didn't drink all day long. She did the same thing every day: sat by the pool, talked on the phone and drank bowlfuls of Bombay Sapphire gin martinis. She was a southern belle who had never been south. My dad's a pretty good guy, but completely out of his depth when it comes to my mom. He would give me money by the envelopeful, mumbling something business-like about The Future while handing over hundred-dollar bills.

This is also when the Duster came along and changed my life. Just thinking about that car makes me feel better.

I'm much steadier walking back towards the table, thank god. It's pretty damn hard to maintain your cool when you can't balance. I slide back into my seat hoping no one noticed that I was in the bathroom for so long.

The first thing I notice is that Spiney is not happy. He's got a grin on his face but it's plastered on there like someone crazy-glued it on. Underneath he looks like he's just been slapped. But before I can ask what's going on, King is standing and has his arm around my waist, introducing me to someone called Dopey.

'Like the dwarf?'

'Nah, man, like the biggest dealer around,' Dopey says and puffs himself up.

'It suits you,' I say. Dopey ignores me and continues the conversation that must have started while I was in the ladies'.

Dopey looks at King who has slid back into his chair. 'So how long has it been for you two?'

I'm just about to tell Dopey that we're not keeping score, but Spiney is looking at me and shaking his head.

'What?' Dopey says.

'You guys want another pitcher?' King stands and pats his pockets for money.

'What's with you, King?' I say, but he's already up at the bar.

Dopey is still looking around at all of us like he's expecting something. Spiney is past looking slapped and has moved on to blank. Sissy is being Sissy.

I attempt a smile at Dopey who is staring at Sissy.

'What?' he says again and then looks at me like I just interrupted him.

I figure that this is going nowhere so I put on my best hostess voice. 'So what do you do now, Dopey? Are you still pushing?' I almost crack up because it sounds so ridiculous to ask that question and sit up straight at the same time.

'Nah,' he says, still staring at Sissy. 'Well maybe, I don't know. I just got out and I'm not too keen to go back.'

'Oh, so you were inside? Did you see King? He was inside for a little while not too long ago.'

God, listen to me, I'm talking like they could have run into each other at a dentist convention in Miami. My mother would be proud.

'Nah, he was in minimum. I was medium.'

Something inside of me wants to squish Dopey like a little bug. Instead I say, 'So how do you know King?'

'High school. We used to do a lot of partying.'

Dopey looks at Sissy and says, 'Man, you and King must be like an old married couple by now. Didn't you start up around twelve years old?'

I look over at Sissy and Spiney. Spiney is still stuck on blank and Sissy is moving her lips but nothing's coming out. I stare at her for a second and wonder if maybe I have finally found the right psychological mix to block her out. All I can hear in the whole bar is the jukebox.

'Excuse me,' I say and wobble to the bathroom again. Unsteady for a whole different reason this time.

I don't go into the stall because all my energy leaves me as soon as the bathroom door closes behind me. It's all I can do to lean against the sink. I look into the mirror and see that Spiney has lent me his slapped expression. I breathe and wonder how long it will take to get to blank.

One little piece of information and everything falls into a different place. I wish that it didn't make sense.

Then Sissy is in the door and it seems my psychological cocktail has worn off because she's at full volume.

'It was a long time ago and high school and everyone knows that high school is a developing stage in people's lives and not part of our complete lives at all and besides who really cares because – '

'Sissy.'

' – it's insignificant. Not at the time but certainly now and –'

'Sissy.'

' – for the rest of time those memories will get smaller and –'

'Sissy.'

' – smaller – '

'Sissy, shut up,' I say and put my hand over her mouth. 'Shut up, Sissy, for once just shut up please.' She stares at me with her big surprised eyes fluttering above where my hand covers her mouth. It looks like her eyes are moving to make up for the stillness of her lips. Then my hand starts to shake and I drop it.

'Shut up, Sissy,' I say. 'Please just this once.'

And miraculously she does.

The way King never seems to mind her constant talking. How the two of them have more stories to tell than the rest of us put together. How Sissy knew exactly what to cook that first night when King came over to my trailer. How she always seems to know a little bit more about King than I do. And how Sissy and Spiney started going out back in the band days.

'Spiney joined the band and you liked him better so you switched?'

She nods again, her eyes fluttering away.

'Shhhhh, Sissy,' I say for good measure. I straighten my hair, reapply lipstick, stand up straight and walk past her.

There was a sign in the back window of the Duster saying $850 OBO. $850 was not even a whole envelope of failing-marriage guilt money from my father. I decided that OBO stood for Officially Buggering Off and before I knew it I was in the lineups for insurance and registration.

I thought I would drive over to the Blue my first night with the car. Someone might ask me, 'Are you going home now?'

'Yep.'

'You need a lift?'

And for the first time I would say no.

I never ended up at the Blue. I pointed the wheels in the right direction a couple of times but I always seemed to miss the turn. The town looked different as I circled around. The houses seemed less imposing when you could speed by them. Everything was a bit friendlier when you could leave.

King is back at the table talking to Dopey about the good old days. Spiney is leaning back in his chair drinking his beer.

'You knew,' I say, and I don't whisper either. Dopey looks at me like he wants me to leave. Spiney ignores him.

'Yeah, you?'

'Nope, no idea.'

'Shitty.'

'Yeah.'

'Sorry, Hazel.'

'It's not your fault, Spiney.'

'Yeah, but I didn't tell you and I should have.'

'Not you, Spiney,' I say.

Sissy is bearing down on us from across the bar. Sissy and King making out in the smoking area at school. Sissy and King at a tailgate party.

King and Dopey are laughing at something together and I can tell that King is trying to look at me without catching my eye. Assessing the damage. Sissy sits down and starts gabbing about the insignificance of history compared to the presence of here and now.

King stares at his beer, not looking at anyone now that Sissy is back at the table, and then he perks up. 'Hey, Dopey,' he says. 'The old band rides again. We have a gig coming up.'

And King looks so happy that Dopey gets a big smile on his face. 'Oh yeah?'

I wait for three breaths, then stand up and walk out of the bar. No one follows.

When I was tired of driving the Duster around town I headed out to the country, then back. Then I circled out to the highway that divided the counties and then back. And then down another side road and a little further into places I didn't recognize and back again.

I could be everywhere in the Duster. There were a lot of in-betweens to investigate. Eventually my drives took up entire nights and whole tanks of gas. Then I got an oil change and tune-up, replaced the blown speakers and drove some more.

Looking at it from this far away, all the way from Even More, I can see that my trips were test drives. Dry runs for my real trip.

One night I drove so far I couldn't think of a single reason to turn back.

I can see my progress as if it's drawn out on a map. Circles surrounded by larger circles and then more circles in more directions – all coming together to form a dizzy pattern that makes beautiful sense if you step away from it. I just kind of spirographed my way into the wide world.

I find the Duster in the parking lot of Old Joe's and sit behind the wheel for a long time. I'm tired. I'm so tired that it's a challenge to turn the key to start the engine, to hit the gas and drive back to the park. I drag myself to bed and pull the covers over my head. I fall asleep.

About four in the morning King and Dopey come in and I wake up. I hear giggling and the fridge door opening and closing and beer cans being shotgunned.

I wish that I had a map of my spirographing. Little push-pins marking all my stops along the way, showing progress.

Egg and I are back in the thrift.

'Does spending so much time here mean we're second-hand goods?' I say.

'No, it means no one appreciates our intrinsic value.'

'Damn right,' I say.

We're playing Trouble. The pop-o-matic bubble is cracked but it still works. I pop it. 'Six.' I move around the board. 'Come to Old Joe's with me?'

'I never go out.'

'Will you, though?'

'I guess, I mean, sure. Sure I will.'

'King is having a gig and I need to fill the house.'

'Oh.'

'What?'

'I don't think I like him, that's all.'

'What are you talking about? How can you not like him? You haven't even met him.'

'Because he doesn't like me.'

'What?'

'I'm a geek, Hazel, let's face it. I like math, for crying out loud, and computers. Your boyfriend beats up people like me.'

'He does not.'

Egg gives me a look and I don't know what to say. Now that I think of it, I can't really see King and Egg getting along. I can kind of see King making fun of Egg. And then I think of this morning, how when I was leaving for work, I had to step over Dopey sprawled out beside the couch. Beside it, like he couldn't even make it the extra foot to actually get onto the couch. And I think of King last night saying, 'Don't worry about it, buddy, stay as long as you want.'

'Look,' I say and take a big breath. 'I would really like to have a friend there that night.'

Egg looks surprised for a moment, starts to say something and then stops. I tell myself that Spiney and Sissy will be there and the gang from around town that always hangs out at Old Joe's will be there. I stare back down at the pop-o-matic. Pop. Pop. Four. Two. I don't say anything and I can tell Egg is looking at me and for some damn reason I feel like crying.

'Oh hell,' I say and finally look up at Egg.

'I'll go, Hazel. I think it would be fun. I really do.'

'Okay,' I say and take a deep breath. We finish our game.

Turns out that there are certificate courses in scuba diving running at the rec centre just a half-hour drive from here. I was lucky because they run only twice a year and I got in just in time. It's almost fall, so most of the people in my class are getting ready to go diving during their luxurious beach vacations. There are a few older couples, and a bunch of other people, like me, who are curious. We are all toes lined up against the edge of the pool – only mine are painted.

On the first day we all introduce ourselves. The instructor tells us to get really comfortable with one another because we will be scuba buddies and, in real water, we would have to depend on each other for our very lives. We all glance around at one another and smile. I try to look like I'm worth saving.

The scuba gear is complicated and the whole diving thing is pretty serious. You have to check the equipment in a certain order and then do a bunch of double-checks. The safety lists and the gear-learning are going to take the first three lessons. 'And that's only if you do your homework,' the instructor keeps saying as he hands out huge binders. 'If you don't get this first part down cold, you can come back for the next class in the spring.' To get a proper scuba-diving licence I have to do a written test and then a practical hands-on test.

I don't mention the scuba lessons to anyone right away. I don't mean to keep it secret or anything, it's just that I want to do this on my own.

I spend the next five days studying. There isn't a whole lot else to do since King is always over at the sinking trailer practising with the band. And then there's Dopey following him everywhere he goes. I swear he was going to follow King into the bathroom yesterday. But at least I can study in peace.

There's this big chapter with lists of things that you have to have memorized backwards and forwards before you even put your gear on – all these safety procedures. You have to have the checklist memorized so well that you can run through it without even trying, or at times when you might be panicking for lack of oxygen or too much adrenalin or coming out of the water too fast or all the other perils that might pop out of nowhere. There's no chapter on sharks.

I'm sitting on the rocker with the binder across my lap reciting the list out loud. And then, before I know it, Sissy is at the front door and staring at the binder. She starts talking about personal goals and how it's important to be practical about your future.

I roll my eyes. 'What's going on, Sissy?'

She stops the personal-goal speech and goes into the reason she came here, never missing a beat. 'You really have nothing to worry about with King. If you are thinking any bad thoughts you can just stop right now because they will only lead you in the wrong direction. I can tell by the way he looks at you that he's madly in love with you. I know it, Hazel – '

The screen door opens again and King is there. I can tell that he heard what Sissy was saying. He looks at me and is about to say something when Dopey is right up behind him asking if there are any cold beers in the fridge. King looks at Sissy and says, 'Deal with this?' And Sissy is right out the door telling Dopey that she thinks there is beer at her house and why doesn't he come over for a visit. Dopey doesn't want to go and starts coming into the trailer again but King shuts the door on him and locks it.

He comes over to the rocking chair, moves the scuba binder to the floor and kneels down in front of me. 'I should have told you,' he says.

'I don't like Dopey,' I say.

'I kind of figured you wouldn't,' he says and laughs. 'I can't really blame you.'

King tells me about the practices with the band and about what he's doing at work. Dopey comes around and bangs on the door. King answers it and steps outside. I can hear Dopey saying, 'Why you gotta be like that, man?' and King comes back in shaking his head and smiling.

He sees me looking at him and hitches his jeans. 'Yep,' he says, trying to look all tough-guy, 'gotta put in some time with the old lady.'

I have memorized a checklist of King. I have to know it so well that I can run through it even when I'm panicking. The list is long but it begins and ends with *I love him*.

The dress rehearsal for the gig is tonight. Actually, I'm not supposed to call it a dress rehearsal. King says that dress rehearsals are theatre stuff and they sure as hell aren't doing theatre – no offence to Kiss, Queen and the Who. It's called a jam.

The other great thing is that Dopey is gone. Just like that. I woke up this morning and didn't have to step over him. When I asked King about it he just shrugged his shoulders and said, 'That's Dopey, he just comes and goes.'

I like the part where he goes.

So the last jam before the gig is tonight. I love band lingo. We're all hanging out in the trailer, Sissy, Spiney, King and I, and also Scotty the singer and the drummer Mo. The night is mostly fun so far.

The guys have decided to wear black. So they're all here in their black Levi's and black T-shirts. King is looking pretty damn great.

'Grab me another beer, will ya, honey?' says Mo for the third time tonight.

I suspect that I'm getting 'honey' because he can't remember my name. I get the beer out of the fridge and throw it to him. Mo has to stop the beer from hitting him and Spiney smiles and shrugs.

King rubs his hands together and then grabs a beer bottle with a flourish and takes a drink. 'Well, kids, are we ready to make the trek?'

The guys stand up right away – they are all under King's command. He is the ringleader because, after all, it was his idea to do a reunion gig.

Sissy comes over and says, 'Hey, Hazel, it looks like this could be good for these guys. It looks like it's a very positive force. I'm glad that they finally have a stage. Everyone needs to get up on their own version of a stage. All the world's a stage and that has never been more true – '

'Cheers, Sissy,' I say.

She grins and says, 'Cheers, baby.'

I put a bunch of beer in a backpack and head out with the group.

The guys walk ahead of us in a big line. They look like old pictures of the Rolling Stones. Sissy and I are the stragglers. Now there's a band name for you, the Stragglers. Sissy goes on about the power that music can have over a person and how humanity should use that power for positive change. I think I've almost forgiven her for not telling me her big secret – that's my power of positive change. At the same time I'm trying to be positive, I'm wondering why I immediately didn't like Scotty and Mo. The same thing happened with Dopey. Scotty, Mo and Dopey definitely have that dinosaur attitude that girls don't count, and when they show up, King and Spiney go right along with it.

This thought makes me feel like turning around and walking back to the trailer just to see if anyone notices. I bet Sissy would just go on talking and the boys would go on walking and I would be long gone.

I take a beer out of my backpack and decide to get drunk. I let Sissy talk the rest of the way so I can drink.

When we get to the trailer, beers are handed out, gear is plugged in and Mo goes out back to 'see a man about a mule.' There is general shuffling and then the noise of everyone tuning and arranging their gear, and then it starts.

Mo hits his drumsticks against one another while he counts to four, and everyone starts in. The music is good once the guys get going. They rewrote a bunch of their songs and they sound even better than the last versions. There's lots of head-nodding signals flying around the room. One nod to say *Come in here*, a chin lift to say *This is where we go back to the bridge*. You can tell that the boys have been playing together for a long time. They hardly have to stop to fix the songs.

Mo's girlfriend made posters for the gig. A couple of them are taped up around the room. The artwork definitely isn't professional – the poster looks like it was done with one of those stencil sets you have in grade school. Every letter is a different pencil-crayon colour. But it does the trick. Time, date and place with 'The Defenders' written in big letters across the top. What the guys think they are defending is still a mystery to me. Defend away, if it makes you happy, that's what I say.

There isn't much room in the trailer, so Sissy and I end up sitting on the floor. Our job is to drink beer and listen and smile and generally be supportive while the guys jam. We are the groupies.

Some of the songs they wrote are really catchy. It's not quite pop, but it's close. Hooky melody lines and, of course, wicked bass lines from King. He's really clever with melody and counter-melody and all that. I'm relieved to hear that there isn't a hint of the former evil-sounding playing. Sissy and I nod our heads and tap our toes along with the beat. We grin at one another from time to time. There isn't much point in talking because the amps are all turned up to eleven. No talking is fine with me.

The guys start on the second run-through of the set. This time there are some rough spots where someone screws up, probably because everyone is drinking a lot of beer. But generally I'm pretty damn pleased with the whole thing. I didn't see the Defenders in their heyday and I have to admit that I was a bit worried that they would suck.

The room started to spin after my last beer and I have to go to the bathroom. I've been trying to hold it for a long time because my choices are walking back to the trailer or peeing in the long grass. But now I have no option, so after the song ends, I get up to go outside. On my way out the door, Mo yells over to me, 'Will you grab me a beer, honey?'

I swear that guy has never said anything to me besides 'Grab me a beer, honey.' I look over at him but don't answer and the guys all go, 'Ohhh, Mo, better get your own beer,' and they laugh.

I stomp down the gangplank and find a good pee spot. I'm squatting down and I realize that I'm pretty drunk now and probably shouldn't drink any more beer. Well, maybe just one more, but slowly. Drunk is definitely working, though, because when I go back into the trailer I'm feeling a bit better.

And then I feel a lot better when I look at King. He's playing with his eyes closed and he's grinning. He looks like pure bliss. This is King. And suddenly I'm really glad I came to this sinking trailer. I knew that I needed to see this but I didn't realize how much.

A really rocking song starts and I hop up and start dancing in my small space. I'm a pretty good dancer so I'm not embarrassed at all. Then Sissy hops up and starts dancing too. The guys yeehoo at us and pick up the tempo. By the time the song comes to an end we are all laughing and Sissy and I are gasping for breath. Perfect fun – finally.

After the set is run through for the second time, the boys toast to the gig and pack up the instruments. I get stuck with doing the cord winding, but it's better than taking apart the drums. Besides, there's a real technique to cord winding and I have it down. You have to roll the cord between your fingers as you wind, otherwise it will get twisted the wrong way and the wires inside could cross. King taught me.

The boys are packing up and grinning at one another like they know that they have just done a really good thing. They talk about the gig that's coming up and then they talk about all the other gigs they could have if they wanted to. And how maybe they should start writing new songs and they should get a four-track in here and see how a recording would turn out. Everyone keeps saying, 'You never know.'

The beer is flowing and I sing little bits of the songs I heard tonight. Spiney says maybe I should be a backup singer and I spin around and sing, 'Doooo wop wop,' and everyone laughs. By the time we get out of the trailer and back into the fresh air I feel like we could all fly home.

We had Sissy and Spiney over tonight. It was crazy fun and a big relief after everything.

We sat around the kitchen table playing cards and talking about anything that came into our heads. Everything is somehow okay between the four of us. It's like we all decided to forget about the Sissy-and-King news and just get on with our lives. We sat around the table for hours, talked a lot and drank a lot of beer. For some reason, every time we finished a beer we just threw the can out the front door. I don't know how it started but all of a sudden it was funny as hell to throw the empties out the door. So now it's really late and Spiney and Sissy have staggered off home. I'm at the table finishing my last beer and King is in the bathroom.

I look out the door to the front lawn. It's a total mess, beer cans hanging in the wildflowers. 'Why the hell did we do that?' I say.

King comes out of the bathroom walking funny because his pants are around his ankles. 'Doing the pants pants dance,' he sings and waggles his butt. 'Pants pants dance.'

'Oh no,' I laugh. 'I never want to see that again.' I cover my eyes but look through my fingers and keep laughing.

'Pants pants dance,' he sings and puts his arms above his head like a ballet dancer and attempts a twirl.

'Stop,' I say. Now I'm laughing so hard I can't take a breath. My side gets a stitch.

King falls over in the middle of a twirl and lands on his butt. He kicks his pants the rest of the way off and one sock comes off too.

‘Oh no, Hazel,’ he laughs. ‘I don’t think I can get back up. I’m old. I think I broke a hip.’

‘Come on,’ I say and pull his arms to help him up. He pulls me down instead and we lie on the floor beside one another.

‘Thank god for you, Hazel.’

‘Tell me why,’ I say. I love it when King gets like this. It’s the closest thing to mushy I’ll ever see.

‘Because,’ he says, ‘look at us. If you weren’t here I would be lying on the floor of this trailer all by myself. Where’s the fun in that?’

‘No fun,’ I say.

‘Or there could be some other gal here,’ he says and raises his eyebrows.

‘Do you want a punch in the nose?’

‘There could be some other gal here, but I would just be annoyed,’ he says. ‘Let’s face it, most gals are annoying. But you’re all right, Hazel.’

‘You’re still verging on a punch in the nose.’

‘You love me,’ he says and throws an arm across me in his drunken version of a hug.

‘Yeah, I guess I do.’

Then King jumps up. ‘I’ll get those cans cleaned up.’ He rubs his hands together.

He finds a plastic bag under the sink and stands in the middle of the kitchen half-naked, weaving back and forth and grinning at me. ‘You really are okay for a chick. You know that, Hazel? We have synchronicity. Same,’ he says and points at himself and then at me. ‘Same on the inside.’

He grins his lopsided grin, nods his head and weaves. Then, just like that, he’s out the front door. T-shirt, one sock and singing a song. ‘You got to know when to hold ’em,’ he sings.

I stand in the doorway and watch him stumble around in the Newfoundland flowers practically naked. I'm half amused and then half horrified because there's a group of people walking down the street. They're trying not to look at him.

'Know when to walk away. Know when to run.'

He's having a grand time, beating out the rhythm of the song with a couple of beer cans. He has almost all the cans crammed into the plastic grocery bag now and is singing his song louder and louder.

'When the dealing's done,' he howls. And then he shakes his butt at the entire street – up and back down.

I look over to the group but they're ignoring the spectacle, thank god. And then in another way I don't care what they think. It's funny. I want to take off my clothes too and not give a damn. I envy King as much as I'm embarrassed.

King grabs the last can and grins at me. 'Got 'em all.' He holds up the bag.

'Yes, you do. Come on, gorgeous,' I say. I smile and hold out my arms.

'I love it when you say stuff like that,' he says and stumbles up the front steps. He drops the bag of cans beside me and half of them roll out and clatter down the steps. 'You know,' he says, 'maybe you should make an honest man outta me, Hazel.'

'Good luck,' I say and pull him inside and close the front door.

King walks straight to the bedroom and crashes on the bed. I put what's left of the bag of empties on the counter. I can hear him struggle with the covers and then he sighs and calls across the trailer, 'You love me, Hazel.'

'Yes I do,' I say, but not loud enough for him to hear. 'Yes I do, you crazy naked drunk guy.'

In the next class, the instructor asks us if we're ready to get our feet wet. Then he brings out the equipment and gets everyone to name all the parts and what they do. I get everything on the first try, including the correct pressures and readings on all the gear.

There are tons of cool little tricks to make diving easier, like spitting in your mask and rinsing it in the water to keep it from fogging up, and pulling your lips around the mouthpiece just the right way so you can breathe without swallowing water.

I thought it would be more like TV: just put on the suit and do that backwards roll into the water. It's not. It's a lot harder than that and you have to be smart about it. Remember the drowning. There's all those warnings about the buddy system and how you have to have someone to go diving with – once you're in the water you always have to be looking for your buddy, checking where they are, so you can keep each other safe. And then, of course, there is a lot of trying to balance the right way and controlling your motion to compensate for the pull of the tank on your back. I know all of this even before I have ever been in a diving suit.

I get dressed in the suit for my first time, including the flippers and mask. When we see each other standing around the pool looking like we're going deep-sea exploring in the shallow end, we laugh.

Then we get in the water and, presto, I'm scuba diving. Or as close as you can get to scuba diving when you're in the middle of town. The instructor was right: the longer I'm in the water, the more the awkwardness of the tank and the equipment goes away.

The pool is a beautiful colour of blue. My classmates look like different beings from underwater – graceful and silent. I swim to the deep end and, as I touch the bottom and turn, I think of how nine-tenths of an iceberg is hidden under the surface.

Before I got the Duster, I swam in my parents' pool a lot. I would dive off the board and swim to the other side, underwater all the way. One day, I opened my eyes underwater and found about a million cocktail olives lying at the bottom of the pool. Mom must have been throwing them in there for weeks. I can still picture her chatting on the phone and, every once in a while, throwing an olive into the pool for conversational emphasis. 'But I just do not believe it. I do – *plunk* – not.' I imagine that perfect olive flying through the air and landing in the cool blue chlorine and I can see why she did it.

I got out of the pool and grabbed the net to scoop out the olives. When I looked down, I couldn't believe that I hadn't noticed them before. They gave the pool an extra green shimmer and the pimentos were the purest red against the perfect aquamarine blue, almost like sea creatures.

Just as I was fishing around for my first catch of green and red, Mom rushed up and pulled me back from the edge. She was hanging off my arm. 'No,' she drawled, acting all wilting-flower in the afternoon sun. 'It's all I have.'

And I swear she was almost crying.

'The pimentos,' I said. And that's all I could get out. I didn't know how to finish. She hugged me and nodded like we understood one another.

That's one of the last things I did at the house. Or, I guess, it's one of the last things I didn't do. People say you only regret the things that you don't do in life, but I don't regret not scooping those olives from the pool. I like that I had a secret with my mom. We were in cahoots, at least for a moment.

The instructor walks along the deck, watching as the class swims up and down the length of the pool. Through the water I can hear his voice filtering down to us, 'You got it! You're doing it! Keep going!' I swim and swim.

Old Joe put up a gig poster on the front door so you know what you're in for as soon as you get to the bar. Walking through the door with that poster on it makes me feel important even though I'm not in the band. It makes the whole gig real.

It's time for sound check. The guys are setting up their instruments on the part of the floor that will be the stage. They put the drums together and set up the amps. Plus, they have already started drinking. Getting a head start on that part of the night too. I catch Spiney draining his beer and say, 'Make sure that you still have enough sober left to hit those guitar strings.' But he just grins, shakes his head and orders another beer. I guess there is something about rock 'n' roll and drinking that just naturally go together.

I'm stuck at a table in the back of the bar writing out the set list so everyone can have their own copy. Mo was supposed to do this, but the more I get to know him the more I suspect that he couldn't write his name on a bathroom wall. I'm using a black Sharpie on a big sheet of white paper so the guys can see the song titles without leaning down and squinting. Their plan is to run the songs together. As soon as they finish one song, they will let the last chord ring out while Mo counts in the next tune and then, bang, they will be into it again.

I'm staring at the makeshift stage thinking that I sure hope Mo's better at counting in the songs than he is at everything else, and then here he comes.

'Hey,' he says and thumps me on the shoulder. 'How's it going … umm … ?'

'Hazel,' I say.

'Oh yeah,' he says. 'I'm Mo.'

'I know.'

'Ha, that rhymes,' he says and walks over to the stage.

I roll my eyes as he climbs behind his kit and starts banging. They are in the real sound-check part of the gig now. The soundman has set up his board behind a section of the bar and he's yelling, 'Tom one.' And Mo hits a tom drum. Then, 'Tom two.'

Bong bong bong.

'Kick.'

Thump thump.

And so on all the way around the kit to the cymbals and cowbell. Then the soundman says, 'Okay, roll it,' and Mo does an old-school drum fill that sounds like something from a past life.

Then it's Spiney's turn and he plays one chord for a second, then fiddles with the dials on his amp. Then he plays the same chord again and fiddles some more. He does that three or four times, then moves on to his guitar pedals.

Sissy is right up front, listening hard. First she stands to the left of the stage and then to the right, then she moves to the back of the bar on the left and then the right. She calls out from each place, 'Oh yeah, Spiney baby, that's really sweet from here, baby.'

I think that's supposed to mean that his guitar tone is good.

Then she gives the sound guy the thumbs-up and a big grin but he ignores her. Now she's back up at the front telling Spiney how great he is. 'You are sending out such good vibrations for this place. There's something in the room for sure. You're really positive, Spiney.'

He's ignoring her too and I wonder for a second what it's like to be Sissy.

I finish copying out the last set list just as King is checking his bass. He hits the low E and lets it ring. He steps on a pedal, hits the E again, adjusts something and then nods at the soundman, who nods back. And that's that.

Scotty is late so the guys order another round and wait for him. I bring over the set lists and pass them out. The guys all take the lists without saying anything and shove them in their back pockets. Mo crumples his up and throws it at his drums. It lands somewhere behind the kit. I look at him and he shrugs and says, 'Then I know where it is.'

I shrug back.

Then he says, 'How many people you guys figure will come tonight?'

'Who knows,' says King. 'I guess we'll find out.'

'What?' says Mo. 'You didn't call everyone?'

'Like who?' says Spiney. 'My mom?'

The guys laugh and then Mo says, 'No, seriously, I called everyone I know just to make sure people show up.'

'They'll show up,' King says. 'We did the posters, right?'

'I still think you guys should get on the phone.'

'Don't worry about it,' King says.

Mo looks at me. 'Did you invite anyone at least? Some chicks or something?'

'No,' I say. But the truth is that I invited everyone I ran into.

Scotty yells from the door, 'Sorry I'm late, guys.' And he goes straight to the stage. 'Is this ready to roll?' He steps up to the mic and says 'check' a couple of times and then he sings a note that is supposed to make him sound cool. I look over to King but he's all wrapped up in the band.

Sissy is bouncing all around the bar again, saying, 'Sounds good from here.'

And then Scotty is swearing into the mic. 'The fucking thing shocked me! There's a short!'

He rubs his lip and glares at the mic. The soundman walks up to the stage and tests it out and, sure enough, there's a short somewhere because he gets a shock too. They look around at all the connections for a while and the guys take turns shutting off their equipment and testing again but nothing works.

Scotty says, 'Do you know how hard it is to sing and put real meaning into the lyrics when you have to worry about your lips touching the fucking mic?'

So they separate all the cords onstage and duct-tape them so they never cross and still the mic sends off a shock. Finally the soundman decides that they should put down a piece of carpet for Scotty to stand on.

Scotty is pouting but he gives the soundman a nod and everyone agrees that the carpet will do the trick.

'Hey, Scotty, why don't you stop drooling on the mic?'

'Fuck off, Mo.'

'Fuck off yourself, why dontcha.'

The guys decide to stay at the bar to play some pool and hang out before the gig. I don't really want to be stuck in the bar from sound check, which started at six, until the gig ends at two or three, so I decide to go home and chill out. Sissy stays, she's happy to watch the boys play pool and drink beer. The groupie thing is fine with her.

I'm pretty excited about tonight. I've never seen the guys play a real gig, and besides, I think it's about time to shake things up a bit. So I pour myself a glass of red wine and take a shower. I stand under the water until the hot runs out and think of how great it will be when I get to scuba dive in the real ocean, somewhere with crazy-coloured fish and seahorses.

I have my getup for tonight all picked out. I got the outfit from the thrift and I jazzed it up a bit. When I showed it to Egg he really loved it. It's a midnight-blue sequined top, kind of like a big elastic tube that I just pull over my head, no sleeves or anything. It looks very 'rich lady from Miami.' On the bottom I'm wearing a faded old jean skirt. And, of course, to finish off my outfit I have to have something flowered, so I'm putting a fake flower in my hair. A blue rose to match everything.

I figure that I have to have big hair to go with this outfit so, after I blow-dry, I plug in my curling iron and get to work. I curl in no particular direction, then I hairspray every inch while I'm holding my head upside down. I put on lots of liquid eyeliner and cherry lip gloss.

I drink my wine with a straw so that I don't mess up the gloss. It's surprising how fast the wine goes when you do that.

I have to pull my top on over my feet and not over my head because I can't sacrifice my hair. Then I put on my skirt and strappy high-heel sandals and take a look in the mirror. Rich seventies porn star from Miami after a day of sailing. Perfect.

When I first get to Old Joe's there are hardly any people. The guys and Sissy are at a table up near the stage and I start to head that way when I see Egg. He's sitting at a table all by himself, just looking around and waiting. He looks really out of place but that just makes me happier to see him.

'Egg! You made it.'

'Of course, yeah of course I did.'

I sit in the chair beside him and grin. 'You like my outfit?'

'Yes, I *still* like your outfit.' He rolls his eyes and I laugh.

'You want a beer or anything?'

Egg gives me a look.

'A Coke? Ginger ale?'

'Coke,' he says, and I go to the bar.

Joe is sitting on a stool behind the bar reading a book. When he sees me he gets up and pours me a beer and I ask for a Coke too.

'Are you worried, Joe?' I say as I look around at the mostly empty bar.

'Nah, these guys could always fill this place and they'll fill it tonight too.'

'I never saw them in the olden days,' I say and smile.

'In the olden days they didn't have electric guitars. Now get out of here, kid.' Joe laughs and waves me away.

Back at the table I give Egg his drink. I tell him that I'll be back in a second and I walk over to King. The band is arguing about something. 'Hi, guys,' I say. And then I stand back and strike a pose, waiting for King's lopsided grin. I can't wait to hear what he has to say about how I look. I keep grinning and posing but no one notices me. 'Hi there, everyone,' I say again and tap King on the shoulder. King turns around with an angry look.

'What the hell time is it?'

'Nine-thirty-ish, I guess.'

'Okay,' he says. 'Let me know when it's ten to ten. I don't have a watch.'

'Me neither,' I say, but he has already turned back to the table. I look at Sissy to try to figure what the hell is going on but she is right in there with the rest of them. They are all talking over one another, no one listening to anyone else. I guess King is nervous.

'Okay,' I say to no one in particular and walk back to Egg.

'Was that him?' Egg says.

'Who?'

'Your boyfriend.'

'Oh yeah.' I look over to where the band is still talking away. 'He's really preoccupied right now or I'd introduce you.'

'It's okay.' Egg shrugs his shoulders. 'You look really great, Hazel. Seventies porn star, right?'

'Yeah.'

'It's okay, Hazel, he's just preoccupied, you said it yourself.'

'Yeah, I know. You're right. So?' I say and smile. 'What are we going to do next week?'

Egg and I talk about new schemes for improving the shop. The place has already started to make more money.

People are starting to come in now. The place still looks pretty empty for a gig but at least the tables are half full and there are a couple of people sitting at the bar. Joe is busy pouring beer. I feel a little bit guilty for not talking to Sissy and for not sitting at the front table. But then I realize that I don't really care.

I tell Egg about my last scuba class. He talks about his impending departure back to school but I ask him to change the subject. 'It's not that I don't care,' I say to him and he nods.

'I know, Hazel. I'm going to miss you too.'

I nod.

His kindness and the thought of not having him around anymore almost makes me cry, so I focus back on the room. It's really filling up now. All the tables and the stools along the bar are full and people are still coming in. This is the most people I have ever seen jammed in here. Joe is going full tilt pouring beers and ringing them up. I decide to pitch in and gather up a bunch of empty bottles and glasses. I drop them in the dish tray behind the bar and order another round. He pours. 'This is on me, Hazel.'

I look over to the band table. The guys are surrounded by people. The gang that's usually here for a good time is out in force tonight. Then I notice that the caps girl is here too. She is standing by King but his back is to her. I decide to not care. I can barely make it back to my table because I have to say hi to so many people but I'm feeling much better now that there's a crowd here.

'Miss Popularity,' Egg smiles.

'Oh shoot,' I say. 'What time is it?'

'Five to.'

'Oh-oh,' I say and run up to the band table. I squish through the crowd to talk to the guys. 'Time to rock 'n' roll,' I tell them.

They are looking excited and nervous at the same time. Whatever they were arguing about before must be settled because now they are slapping each other on the back, buddies all around.

King stands up and grins at the band. 'Well,' he says, 'let's do it up.'

Sissy takes out her camera. 'I'm going to capture the moment,' she says. 'Because there will be a time when we all look back on this and find that there is something to learn.'

'You know it, Sissy,' I say and stop listening. Sissy is all caught up in her camera so I go back to the table.

'The moment of truth,' I say to Egg and rub my hands together. The lights over the dance floor come on and the blue sequins on my top reflect all over the room.

'Cool,' says Egg. 'Did you plan that?'

And right then the music begins.

The first song has a drum lead-in that starts so abruptly it makes everyone jump. Then the rest of the band comes crashing in. This is one of the songs that I like. I look over at Egg, who's watching and nodding his head.

Scotty is pretty drunk and he's kind of weaving while he sings – I wonder if it's an act. And, of course, there's King playing bass for all he's worth. He looks like he's in a different world. His eyes are closed and he's moving his head up and down to the beat, throwing his shoulders into it.

The first song finishes and everyone claps like mad. And then, just like they planned, the band starts right into the next song. More people are standing up front now, holding their beers and listening. Some people sway back and forth with the music like they could start dancing any second. I figure that if people dance, the gig can be chalked up as a success.

'Will you dance?' I ask Egg when there's a quiet spot in the music. He gives me a funny look like I should know better. 'Okay, okay,' I say and we laugh.

Sissy is up front snapping away. She crouches down in front of Spiney and takes pictures and then moves on to King and finally stands in the middle of the room and takes a picture of the band. The whole time she is moving her lips.

People are starting to dance a little now. A couple of girls up front have cleared a patch and they're swaying to the music. Sissy gives them a dirty look for getting in her way but she backs off and runs over to say something to the soundman. A slow song comes on and some couples go out to dance. It's a pretty good song, the one I couldn't get out of my head before.

And then, before I can stop myself, I'm scanning the room for the caps girl. I look down at the table quickly. It doesn't matter, I tell myself and run through the scuba checklist to keep my mind busy.

I like the next song and I guess King does too because he's got his eyes closed and his head thrown back. He looks like he's feeling the song as much as he's playing it. Seeing him like this makes me breathe deeper than I have since that night on the roof. It seems like this smoky old bar has better air than the rest of the world tonight.

The set ends and everyone claps and shouts. Egg and I cheers one another and I get up to get King a beer. I figure he could use one after that set.

When I find him he is surrounded by people. When I finally make my way through I say, 'Hi, gorgeous,' and hand him the beer.

He drinks half of it in one long swallow and says, 'Thanks, I needed that.'

'You were great.'

'Oh yeah?' He smiles and smiles. A couple of people thump him on the back and congratulate him. One guy asks if they are going to play 'Roses.'

'I almost forgot about that song,' says King. 'Thanks, buddy.'

'Well, I guess I better let you back to your fans,' I say.

King kisses the top of my head, then frowns and wipes his mouth. 'Lots of hairspray tonight, Hazel.'

'Seventies porn star,' I say. But he has already turned away and some other guy is standing where King was.

The other guy says, 'No way, you're too young.'

When I get back to the table Egg asks, 'How's the rock star?'

'Rockin,'' I say.

After a while the guys get back up onstage, tune their instruments and flick switches. People in the crowd quiet down, waiting for the music. Some people who were at the back of the bar move up to the front. Mo starts up on the drums with a sudden bang but no one joins him. Mo comes to a halt and the band glares at him. 'Sorry,' he says.

'Even I know that was the last set,' says Egg, looking proud of himself for figuring it out.

The band is standing onstage looking uncomfortable. King yells something out, Mo counts them in and they are back on track. At first the audience doesn't do anything, as though they're waiting for the band to screw up again, but when they go full steam ahead everyone starts swaying and nodding their heads to the music. I can see the beginning of stress from King but it goes away by the time they reach the chorus of the next song.

'Fuck!' Scotty yells into the microphone. He's holding his mouth and glaring at the soundman. The band keeps playing and repeats the chorus so he can come back in and get going with the song again. Scotty is still glaring at the soundman but he sings and the crowd continues nodding.

My top sparkles in the disco light as I turn around to watch King again. Even Egg is getting into it now. I'm practically busting to dance. When the next song comes on and picks up momentum I look over to Egg and ask if he would mind, and just like that I'm up on the dance floor.

I stand still for just a second and feel the vibrations of the bass come through the air and into my chest. I can feel every note King plays. Soon nothing else exists but the music and dancing. My body shifts into a different mode and I am completely with the music. I close my eyes to get even more into it and then there's Scotty swearing into the microphone again.

Scotty kicks the mic stand and it comes crashing down into the audience. I jump aside and it lands beside my feet. 'Holy,' I say, dazed.

The music fumbles around a bit. Mo has stopped playing and King and Spiney try to improvise and fill in the song, just the two of them. King glares at Mo and Mo starts playing again, but he's off the beat. The guys sync up with him and now it's obvious that there's no singer.

I move back to the table, my eyes on King the whole time. He is glaring at Scotty and Mo and at anything else that gets in his way. Scotty picks up the microphone stand and touches the mic a couple of times, checking to see if it will shock him.

I sit down beside Egg and we look at one another. The guys have started into an improvisation to try to save face. It's horrible. King is playing his fast and angry notes and the rest of the guys are trying to catch up, just like the time I heard them in the sinking trailer. Scotty is over yelling at the soundman and I can't even look at the stage. A lot of the people who were up front are moving backwards, walking away and finding chairs.

The soundman turns down the volume and then cuts the power to the stage. All we hear for a second is Mo smashing away at the drums, out of time. The drums stop and the soundman says that there will be an intermission. In the quiet we can hear him swearing at Scotty.

'Oh shit,' I say and look at Egg. 'Shit. Shit. Shit. Shit.'

'Five swears, Hazel? That must be bad,' Egg says, trying to make me laugh. When I don't, he says, 'Maybe you should get up there?'

I look over and Egg shrugs his shoulders. He looks like he would like to say something but doesn't know what. And neither do I.

'Okay.' I nod to Egg and stand up. I square my shoulders as I make my way through the people. Sissy is sitting alone at the front table packing up her camera. She isn't talking at all. I put my hand on her shoulder and she smiles up at me. I can tell she's upset.

'They should have practised more,' she says and she looks down.

A lot of people have sat back down but there are some stragglers up at the front. A couple of guys are asking if there's anything they can do and asking if the wires are insulated. King is standing beside his amp, kicking it over and over again and talking to Spiney. All I can hear is 'bullshit this' and 'bullshit that.'

I wave at Spiney who has caught sight of me. He looks at me and shakes his head. Then King is looking at me. 'What?' he says.

'Nothing.'

'Good.'

And that's all I hear before I turn around and head back, but not before I hear King say, 'Bunch of amateurs. What the hell was I thinking? Bullshit.'

I make my way back to the table. Lots of people are leaving and the house music comes back on. I can hear people asking one another if there's going to be another set and one guy I don't recognize says, 'I hope not.'

'Let's get out of here,' I say to Egg.

I feel ridiculous in my outfit. I can tell my hair is falling down and looking stupid now. I've lost the blue flower. I'm not feeling Miami at all, more like pathetic slut teenager.

We get up quickly and leave. I'm relieved to be out of the bar and I can tell Egg is too.

'It wasn't that bad,' says Egg. 'Mostly it was good.'

I just shake my head. I don't know what to say.

'Want to get some pizza?' he says. He's looking apologetic and it makes me feel worse because he's been nothing but great tonight.

'I should go home and wait for King.'

'You don't have to.'

'Yes I do,' I say. I look at him standing there feeling sorry for me. 'Besides, I'm really tired.'

He nods at me and smiles. He's doesn't believe me but lets me get away with it. We say goodbye and I walk across the street to where there's a taxi waiting. 'The park,' I say. And before I even realize that I've gotten in, I'm heading back to Even More.

I look in the mirror. Black is streaked down my face from where I'm trying to rub off all the liquid eyeliner. I take a close look, lean right in and stare at myself for a good long time. There are black circles under my eyes and they aren't left over from the makeup. The longer I look, the more my face starts to change – soon I'm staring at a stranger.

I throw my clothes into the corner and try to make my hair calm down, then I put on a huge T-shirt that I wear around the trailer when I'm hungover. I'm standing in the middle of the living room thinking of all the things I'm trying not to think about when King gets home.

He opens the front door, takes a step into the trailer and then stops and looks at me. His shoulders are hunched and he's carrying a bottle of beer. He doesn't say anything. We stand and stare at one another. There's an expression on his face that I don't understand. I can't seem to look right at him and I can't look away either. Suddenly this whole night feels like it was my fault. Then, just like that, he turns and walks back out the door. It slams. I stand very still and listen to his shoes hit the front steps and then nothing.

He's gone.

After two days King is back and after two more days he's speaking to me again, but I wish that he would go back to not saying a thing. The scuba lessons are taking a lot of my time. Maybe that's what's bugging him. He hates that I'm scubaing and, to tell you the truth, I don't really care why.

Egg and I have been hanging out at the thrift almost every day. We never mention the gig night or the fact that I never want to go home after work. We spend a lot of time going over the questions that will be on my diving test. Egg is a great study partner. Of course he is. He asks things like 'What is the optimum reading on the tank pressure valve and what unit of measurement is it in?' And when I answer I can tell right away if I got it right because he gets this look on his face like he's trying not to smile. When we go through the list four times in a row and I get all the answers right on the first try, he gets the trying-not-to-smile look times ten.

'So, Hazel,' says Egg. 'What's next?'

'What do you mean?'

'I mean once you get the scuba diving aced, then what? Truck driving?'

'Or how about getting my pilot's licence?' I say.

'Well? What's it going to be?'

'I don't know.'

I'm stuck for a minute thinking about breathing underwater and living a life where I take vacations. I take a deep breath. 'I don't know,' I say again.

On my way home, all I can think about is the licence and actually seeing something underwater besides the bottom of the rec-centre pool. I'm thinking reefs and starfish, electric eels and manta rays. I'm thinking shipwrecks and sunken treasure.

I park the Duster out front of the trailer and I think about the scariest part of diving, the claustrophobia. You have to be really confident in the water because sometimes, with all the pressure crushing down on you, it's easy to feel like you can't take a breath, like you can't get to the surface. Those are the times when you have to tell yourself that it's okay, that you can breathe and that everything is going to be okay because you are checking your gauges for air and your compass for direction. You have to believe and then everything gets easier. If you second-guess yourself you are lost.

King is on the front steps. 'Hey,' I call out to him. 'I almost have my certificate. Cool, huh?'

'Ahhh, the scuba licence,' he says.

There is something weird in his voice, and I don't like it. 'The scuba licence,' he says again and makes the word 'scuba' sound ridiculous. 'Good thing you're getting that certificate, Hazel,' he says. 'Good thing.'

'Why?'

'Because you never know, do you?'

'What don't I know?'

He throws his empty beer can onto the ground and opens another one. 'You just never know,' King says.

He's smiling, but it's not a happy smile. He's drunk, drunker than I've seen him in a long time. And he's mean. He doesn't get mean like Sissy gets mean. King will never come right out and say what's getting to him. His is a beating-around-the-bush mean.

'I guess no one ever really knows,' I say. And I walk right past him into the trailer.

When you're under the water, and there are strange creatures all around you, it's important to know exactly what you are doing. Keep your breathing calm. Trust yourself. Navigate.

Sissy hit Spiney.

Even More just got even more crazy.

Spiney's sitting in our kitchen right now. 'It's just like a damn Three Stooges movie,' he says. He keeps rubbing his head like he's thinking, but it's because there are three big bumps there. 'People don't do this kind of shit.'

King is trying not to laugh, but he can't help it, and when a laugh slips out he says, 'Sorry, man.'

Spiney says, 'What the hell is funny here?'

'I don't know,' says King. 'I mean Sissy … Sissy is … It's crazy, man.'

'Bugger off,' says Spiney. 'You say this is crazy but I could see it coming.'

'Come on, Spiney, Sissy is okay,' I say.

For some reason I feel like I have to stick up for her, but she did hit him, so I'm not sure why I'm in for the defence.

'No way,' he says. 'There's some evil in her.'

'Come on! You sound like a comic book.'

Spiney washes down aspirin with beer. 'Well,' he says, 'the whole thing was like a damn comic book. I mean she was just sitting there talking like always.'

King and I say 'like always' along with him.

'And then in the middle of a sentence she walks away. Whatever, right? I don't think anything of it. I can't remember what the hell she was saying. You know how it is.'

We nod that we know.

'I'm putting new strings on my guitar and then *wham wham wham*! Three times!' He holds up three fingers.

King says, 'Why didn't you stop her after the first one?'

'I was putting strings on my guitar! What was I supposed to do? Hold it up above my head to block the frying pan?'

King starts to laugh again, and to tell the truth I want to laugh too, but it's not really funny.

'Thanks,' Spiney says. 'Fine, that's the last time I talk to you about anything.'

'But a frying pan,' says King. 'That's classic.'

'Bugger off, will you? Listen, here's the strange part … after she hits me, you know what?'

'What?'

'She sits down and looks at me.'

'What did she say?'

'That's just it,' says Spiney. 'Nothing. She didn't say a goddamned thing. She just sat and looked at me for a while and then when I got up she nodded her head once. That's it, no talking, and it lasted at least two minutes. Did you ever hear Sissy not talk for two minutes? I go to sleep and she's talking. I wake up and she's talking. Her not talking scared the damn wits outta me.'

'Jesus,' says King.

'Bugger off,' says Spiney.

'You think I should go over there?' I look at Spiney, and he rubs his head.

'No, I don't think so. She needs this. I mean, bugger, screw it. Whatever. You know?'

'Sure,' I say.

I get up and bring the guys another round of beer. I take one for myself and go sit on the front step. From here, I can see Sissy and Spiney's trailer.

The day is a bit windy and there is some dust in the air. When you're looking through dust you get the illusion that things are further away than they really are. It's a weird trick that your eyes play on you – something about how we're always unconsciously judging distance. When you look at faraway things, you have to factor in the state of the air. I've heard that explorers got all messed up by that when they first saw the Rocky Mountains. They didn't judge the air. The cleaner the air, the closer things look. I guess the air was pretty clear back in the exploring days because those guys thought they could walk across the prairies in just a couple of days. They didn't make it.

I sit for a while and stare at Sissy and Spiney's trailer. It looks far away and feels so close. The opposite of how the mountains must have looked, but every bit as rocky.

The thing I couldn't tell Spiney is that it all kind of makes sense. Sissy is the one who always keeps us from fighting. Think of the caps girl, think of a million times before and since then. It's always Sissy breaking up the problem. She jumps into the action so that nothing gets out of hand. She's the one always telling us to say our words out of love and not out of anger and all that.

Sure, sometimes we don't listen to her. Mostly we don't listen to her. But if anything goes wrong, she's right there. That's what Sissy always has to do, so of course that's where she breaks, right along her strongest part.

After a while I get up and go in for another beer. The guys are talking about what they always talk about: guitars, music, engines. Spiney is back to his normal self of hardly saying anything at all. King is excited. He's saying, 'I know what you need, man, a road trip. We should get on our bikes and bugger off. We can take a week or so and head for the coast. Take a guitar and a tent. What do you say? It would be great, and we could get away from this crap.'

He goes on, but that's the last I hear as I grab another beer and let the front door slam behind me. For a second I feel like I'm in one of those madhouse attractions at a travelling circus where the floor is crooked, where you are never sure where to put your foot for your next step. The feeling freezes me, and then my foot comes down.

I walk over to Sissy's. I can see her through the window. She's doing dishes and talking on the phone. I wave, and she rolls her eyes and makes the talk-talk gesture with dish-sudsy fingers. I nod at her and keep walking.

The beer feels really good in my hand. I like how the cool and the wet of it are exactly the opposite of this dusty day. I take a long drink and head down the road.

I'm out of the park now, going down the highway. Walking along the side of the road on a dusty day isn't the best thing in the world, but it's easy because it means I don't have to make decisions about where to turn. Decisions are the last thing I want to be bothered with right now.

When I first got my Duster, it overheated all the time. I didn't really care because I was never in a hurry to get anywhere. When it got too hot, I would just pull over, pop the hood and let it cool down. The cool-down was a good time to look around at all the things I would have missed if I had just sped on past.

But then people started to say, 'Hazel, I saw you pulled over on the side of the road again.' And everyone would laugh and someone would say, 'Why don't you get that radiator fixed?'

They said it so much that I started thinking, Yeah, maybe I should get it fixed. Especially with King there saying, 'Hazel, this is getting embarrassing, I'm supposed to be a mechanic.'

So I got a new rad and King fixed the Duster. Everything was fine for a while but then the hoses blew and then the manifold cracked. See, if the whole car is old and all the parts are old, then everything will run along together just fine. But I put in a new rad and gave the car a strong point. That's why the hoses went. That's why the manifold cracked. The weak things in the car couldn't stand up to the new strong parts, so they broke. They had to.

I decide that I don't have to go back to the trailer any time soon so I keep walking. I think about all the ways that things can break and all the reasons. I think of how good things can turn bad without you even noticing. And I think about all the things that I have been trying not to notice for a while now: the manifold, the frying pan, the scuba lessons, the mean music – everything trucks around in my head.

I figure that I don't really know what my strongest part is. I can't quite pin it down. I don't really have a mission for peace like Sissy or a mission for calm like Spiney. Then I stop cold. I stop because I realize that I know King's strength. I know it like I know my own name. King's strength is his knack for being the person everyone wants to be, and that scares me. I don't know what his strength is resting on. I'm afraid that it will break and I'm afraid of what it will take with it.

I don't want to go back to the trailer because that would only mean trouble. I don't want to visit with Sissy or Spiney or even Egg. For the last couple of hours I've been sitting in a ditch. I made up a song about sitting in a ditch but the more I sang it the more depressing it got, so I stopped. The last couple of words from my song are still hanging in the air. The words belong to Old Joe – 'When there's nowhere to go, you've found your home.' The words echo around the ditch, becoming heavier and heavier. Then they land right in my lap and there's nothing to do about it.

I have to go somewhere and do something or I'm going to implode. Then I remember the painting I was going to do at the thrift a million years ago. I could paint and get good and tired and then crash out right there. King would worry where I got to and he would realize that he's been a total jerk lately and he would say, 'Hazel, what have I done? Can you ever forgive me? I don't really want to go on that stupid road trip.' And that would be that.

So I go.

I let myself in the back door of the shop and leave the lights off. The thrift looks slightly creepy at night but I know the place so well that I'm not afraid. I make my way through the racks and the shelves to the front of the store.

Then I grab the staple gun from under the counter and staple a big heavy wool blanket over the front window so no one will look in and wonder what the hell I'm doing.

I stop for a second and take a look around. I guess I've never been here after sunset. The whole place feels dusty and old but it also feels like a hideout. I'm playing hide-and-seek with the whole town. I hear cars go by and people on the street walking and talking. They have no idea that behind the blanket in the thrift window is me, Hazel. I guess that makes me home free. I feel dangerous and sneaky.

I turn on some lights and get started. I find the paint cans in the back along with some brushes. I don't have the right kind of brushes but I've never really been a sucker for the right kind of anything. This will work just fine. I move all the racks away from the back wall to clear a space.

I can't move around in the dress that I have on so I change. I strip down right there in the thrift, so I'm buck-naked. I walk around the store a bit getting a feel for this naked thing. I figure that somehow this must be illegal. This is what King must feel like when he walks around in his own skin, clothes or no clothes.

Shirtsleeves and thrift-shop air brush against my skin and I feel like I own this place. Maybe I am the only person who has ever been naked in this room. I prance around a bit and get close to the window. What if the staples don't hold? How's that for a window display? King would do it, I bet.

I take another step closer and I can feel the cool air from the window wash over my feet. King would walk right up to the blanket, take it by one corner and just rip it away. He would be standing there, hands on hips, daring anyone to disapprove. I reach out and touch the blanket and feel its rough wool edge. Then I get a powerful eerie feeling and scamper to the back of the store. It's the same sort of creeps that I sometimes get when I'm holding something really delicate. Like I might bring destruction with just the slightest wrong move. As if I don't know how to touch lightly enough.

The creepy destruction shivers make me cold so I rummage through the men's rack until I find a big white shirt to put on.

The 'go home' song from sitting in the ditch is stuck in my head again so I turn on the radio. The dial is still stuck on the oldies station and that's just fine with me. 'Let's go to the hop, oh baby, let's go to the hop.' I dip my brush into the sage-green paint and start the trim. I can already see how the paint will make a big difference in here. And it feels good to do some physical work. I get serious about the painting and focus on the strokes. Smooth and even up, smooth and even down and dip the brush.

I bet King is wondering where I am by now. It's getting kind of late. Ever since the gig we've been playing this top-secret game called Who Can Stay Away from the Trailer the Longest? It's so secret that the two of us can't even talk about it. The rules are easy: the person who gets home first loses. The person who stays out the latest is obviously having a great time.

I stayed out at Old Joe's until closing the other night and I took my time about getting home too. I thought for sure I would walk in and find King sleeping, but I was wrong. He wasn't there at all. I lost. At the time I thought that I would probably always lose. But not tonight, boy. Tonight I'm not coming home at all.

I'm done the trim so I attack the rest of the wall. I wish I had a roller but thrift-store clerks and beggars can't be choosers. Long smooth and even up, and long smooth and even down.

I mean, what the hell does King think is going on with us anyway? It surprises me in a rotten sort of way that I have no idea what this whole thing looks like to him.

I'm done painting the green so I pick out another paint can, Cape Cod blue, and start the second wall. The radio plays as I shake the new can. 'Yes, I'm the great pretender.' I howl along to the music, 'Ooooh ooooh.' I'm glad I'm wearing only this big shirt because I'm getting pretty damn hot.

My mom sang this song to me once. My parents were having a house party. I was about six at the time. I was supposed to be sleeping but I was sitting at the top of the steps watching all the guests. My parents give a good party. There was hired help walking around with plates of food and bottles of wine. My mom presided over the whole affair, floating around the room smiling and making people laugh. It was like she was this one sparkle that touched everyone in the room.

She really was beautiful, like a movie star. It's hard to believe that she was a mother at all, let alone my mother. I couldn't take my eyes off her.

She floated up the stairs to me and shooed me back into my room. She sang as she climbed the stairs. 'Oh yes, I'm the great pretender, ooh ooh.' She sang as she followed me into my room and lifted the covers on my bed so I could crawl in.

I think of my mom pretending that night. The perfect hostess, the perfect mother and wife. But underneath there's an entirely different person. I think about the outsides and insides of people and wonder which one is real. Some people change their hair colour. Chameleons change according to their surroundings. Other people change everything about themselves and it barely makes a difference. We could all use a fresh coat of paint every once in a while. I hum along with the music and get lost in the paint. Smooth up and smooth down, the gloss of it mesmerizes me – at this moment, despite everything, the world is a beautiful place. I feel myself soaking into the Cape Cod blue.

Time passes.

Someone pounds against the back door like they are going to beat it down. And then they do. The flimsy lock gives way and the door comes flying open, two cops stumbling in after it. I stare at them but I can't say a thing. I don't know how long I've been painting. Daylight streams in through the door and the paint on my brush is dry. I stand and wait until they see me. And they do quickly enough. They see a crazy half-naked chick standing in the middle of the room dazed and covered in paint. Half-naked.

I run for the closest rack of pants and start reaching out for a pair but one of the cops grabs my wrists and tries to hold my hands behind my back. 'Hold on a second,' I yell. 'Hold on a second.'

And that's just what he does – holds – tighter and tighter. I want to kick him away but I'm afraid that would give them a clear view under my shirt so I struggle and throw myself into the nearest rack.

I fall right into the middle of a round clothes rack and something stabs into the back of my leg, a sharp something that takes my breath away.

The younger cop says, 'Hey, she's not wearing pants.' He sounds like he can't decide if he should laugh.

The older one tries to help me out of the rack. He reaches out to me, looking sad, confused and mad all at the same time. He holds out his hand and says, 'Come on, we have to get you out of there.'

'I'm stuck,' I say. And I really am. I twist around and look down through the clothes to see the back of my thigh. The sharp thing I can feel is the hooked end of a wire coat hanger. It's sunk into my leg.

'What the hell?' I say. And that's all I remember.

After I come to, the cops drive me to emergency. I have to lie face down in the back of the police car on the way to the hospital. The young cop drives and the old cop leans over the front seat and holds on to the hanger that's still sticking out of my leg, trying to stop it from moving around. Me, in the back seat of a car, again.

It seems that someone heard noises from the thrift and thought the place was being robbed. What kind of idiot would rob a thrift shop?

The hanger gets pulled out of my leg and I throw up. Then I get stitches. Dissolving stitches on the inside on two different levels and more stitches on the outside. Then I get a tetanus shot, which isn't as bad as people make it out to be. Finally, I get a ride back to the trailer in the cop car. The younger cop says, 'You're just lucky we aren't going to press charges, young lady.'

The older one says, 'Lay off her, will you?'

'She's one of those from the trailer park.'

'Lay off her.'

While I'm listening to them I'm trying to make up my mind if I want to tell them that I'm not from the park, not really. I feel sick and I realize that I don't care enough to bother saying anything. I spend the rest of the ride vaguely wondering if I'm going to throw up in the back of the police car.

When the cop car pulls up in front of my trailer the only thing I'm thinking is, *Please don't let anyone see me*. The older cop offers to help me get to the front door but I shake my head. I manage to hoist myself out of the car. This takes a while. I still don't have any pants on and I'm afraid that the hospital gown they traded for the white shirt will come undone. The young cop sits up front and sighs because I'm taking too long to get out. As soon as I'm on my feet I can hear him complaining about people like me. I don't stick around to listen.

Please don't let anyone see me. I limp through the wildflowers, up the front steps and straight to the couch. I have to lie belly down because of the hole in my leg.

King isn't home yet and I lose again.

Nothing happens.

The police don't call the house and they don't call the thrift either. I get off scot-free – except for the hole in my leg. I spent the last two days on the couch waiting to hear that I should go down to the police station because I was 'one of those from the trailer park' and the cops decided that I shouldn't get a break after all. I waited for someone from the town council to call and tell me that I shouldn't bother to show up for work and don't come near the store ever again. But there was nothing.

And the other truly great thing is that besides the two cops and me, no one knows what happened. I called Egg to see if he could cover my days at the thrift. I told him that I started painting and pulled a muscle. When he came over to pick up the keys, I was waiting on the front step with a big smile and a little lie. I didn't move the whole time he was here so that he wouldn't see me limp. So that he wouldn't ask, 'Hey, Hazel, how did you pull your leg so badly, just from painting?' And so I wouldn't have to say, 'Actually, Egg, I got a hanger stuck in it when I was trying to hide my bare bottom from the cops who were chasing me.'

I am an idiot, but I am an idiot in secret.

I've been on the couch for two days straight, with my favourite blanket thrown over my lap, and I'm starting to go crazy. I'm getting bored with sitting around all day and all night. But the thing that's really driving me crazy is that King hasn't noticed. He hasn't said a thing about how I never move from the couch. Every day I wait until he is out of the house and on his way to work and every night I wait until he is asleep before I limp to the bathroom or change my bandages. He hasn't even said anything about how we aren't sleeping in the same bed.

I have a paper bag tucked under the couch with all the stuff that I got from the hospital pharmacy. Bandages, peroxide and gauze. As soon as King leaves, I pull out the kit and make the change. There is a huge green, purple and yellow bruise around the place where the hanger went in. I didn't see the bruise until this morning because I couldn't bend my leg enough to get a good look at it. But I saw the whole mess today and now I wish I hadn't looked. Seeing that bruise made the other night real in a way the pain did not. Seeing that bruise made me realize some other things too.

I'm not the type of girl who gets picked up by the police. I don't know who this girl is but she sure as hell isn't Hazel or the me that came before Hazel either. This strange girl is afraid of getting caught and afraid of talking to King and afraid of going to work. She's afraid of everything except staying on the couch for the rest of her life. And, come to think of it, that's pretty damn scary too.

I'm putting peroxide on my leg and watching it bubble when I hear King's motorcycle out front. There's no time to put on a new bandage so I cram everything back into the paper bag and shove it under the couch. I just get the blanket over my leg when the front door opens and there's King. Now I have to hold my leg a bit above the couch so that it won't touch and bleed all over everything. I can feel the stitches pulling every time I move even a little bit. I'm trying to find the least painful way to do this and look natural when King looks over at me and nods and says, 'Hazel.'

'King.'

He nods again and goes to the fridge. I try to straighten my leg a bit so it can rest and not hurt so much like it's doing now. King comes back into the room and sits in the rocking chair with his beer. I freeze and try to look like someone who's not in excruciating pain.

'How is Spiney doing?' I ask.

'Okay. He's good.'

'How's his head?'

'Head is good too,' he says and rocks and takes a drink of beer. 'I was thinking of going out to Old Joe's tonight.'

'Oh, you go ahead, I don't really feel like it.'

'Yeah.'

'Yeah what?' I ask.

'Yeah, I guess I wasn't inviting you. I was more like making sure that you weren't going to go there too.'

'Oh.'

'I want to go out on my own, you know? Go out and drink beer and not have to worry about relationship stuff.'

'Wow, I didn't know that I was so much no fun.'

'You are usually. Usually you're okay, but I want a different kind of fun tonight.'

'Oh.'

King finishes his beer in one long swallow and stands up. 'Well then,' he says and knocks the dirt off his jeans. 'Shower time.'

When I hear the shower burst on I grab the kit and smack on a new bandage. I'm so panicked that I do a really messy job and bunch up the tape the wrong way, but it will hold until King gets out of the house. I really should peroxide all over again but I don't have the time. There's a bit of blood on the couch from where I was straining the stitches but it's no big deal.

I shove everything back under the couch and see that there's hardly any blood on the couch because it all landed on the blanket that was wrapped around my leg. I get up, straighten my dress and hobble over to the sink with the blanket and the lousy falling-off bandage and I put the worst of the blood under the cold-water tap. I can't turn the tap on very much because then King will get scalded in the shower and I will get the 'What the hell are you doing out there, Hazel?' yell. So I turn the water on just a trickle and listen. He's not swearing so I'm okay.

There isn't enough water to do a good job and I can't turn the tap any more – I'm stuck. The shower shuts off and I try to squeeze the blanket dry enough to get me back on the couch looking innocent. King is right behind me.

'What happened here?'

He's dripping wet and goddamn he looks good. Buck-naked King is a good King indeed. I can't stop staring so I turn back towards the sink and hope that my dress covers the bandage on my leg. But I feel like he can see through my dress and see through everything else too so I turn back towards him. I don't know what to say. I just keep staring at naked him.

'What happened?' he says again and reaches for another beer like he has all the time in the world to stand around asking me questions. He takes a long drink and stares at me and then at the blanket that's dripping pink all over the kitchen.

'Hmmm,' I say and stall for time because I have no idea what else to say. 'Hmmm,' I say again. 'Well, it's kind of embarrassing really.'

'Oh, forget it. Girl stuff. Forget I asked.'

'Yeah,' I say and turn back to the sink.

I can't stay standing for much longer. I can feel blood running out from under my bandage so I finish twisting the water out of the blanket while King stands around and drinks his beer. I stall as long as I can, wringing and wringing, and then there's nothing else to do but make it to the closest chair. So I reach into the fridge beside me, grab a beer and limp over to the chair at the kitchen table. He doesn't notice.

I take a drink. 'So I'm sure you'll have fun tonight. Are you going with Spiney?'

Half of me doesn't care what he says because I'm so relieved to be sitting. All the standing was pulling my leg and hurting like mad.

'No, he doesn't feel like going out.'

'Sorry, what did you say?'

'Spiney doesn't feel like going out,' he says and looks at me suspiciously.

'The band guys?'

'Hazel, why are you being so nosy?'

'Am I?'

'Yeah, jeez, you are. Can't I just go out by myself for once?'

I'm trying to get comfortable on the chair and not really listening to this stupid conversation. 'Yeah, sure, I was just thinking that you going to Old Joe's without Spiney is kind of strange, that's all.'

'Oh, so now you don't want me to go.'

'No, go. It's fine, whatever you want.'

'Damn right whatever I want. Sometimes I feel like you have me under a microscope.'

'Well, you aren't, so don't worry about it.'

'You worry too much. You know that?'

'No, this is brand-new knowledge.'

'Everything is relationship relationship relationship with you.'

'Hmmm.'

'Maybe you should just chill out for a bit, Hazel. It's not the biggest thing in the world, you know.'

'Yeah,' I say and look up at him. 'You're right, it isn't the biggest.'

And I guess I kind of look at King's nakedness, give him the up-and-down check-it-out glance because King's face goes dark in that mean way that he has and he says, 'You are really a bitch sometimes, Hazel. You really are.'

And just like that, King throws his beer bottle at me. I have to hold up my arms and use the blanket as a shield. I can feel the bottle hit my arm and the beer soak into the blanket and pool around my feet with everything else. When I lower my arms again King is out of the room.

I can't think.

I limp to the counter and my hands shake as I put the whole blanket in the sink. I'm standing in a puddle of beer. I hear King get his stuff together, then walk through the living room. He grabs his spare motorcycle helmet, the one he said was for me, and is out the door. The last thing I hear is, 'That's real nice, Hazel. Real sweet.'

The motorcycle roars down the street and he's gone. I get myself to a chair. My leg really hurts from all this moving around. I take a drink of beer but it tastes like rust. I might throw up.

Who is this Hazel who gets hit by beer bottles? Who is this King who throws them at her?

Here's how it goes. I get brought home by the cops. I sit on the couch. I get hit by a beer bottle. And then what? I go to the pen? Is that the natural progression of things?

I remember this feeling. I had this feeling once before.

I was about twelve or thirteen and I was practising diving in the pool in my parents' backyard. I was diving and my mom and dad were sitting on the deck. Dad was reading the paper and Mom was doing her nails the most perfect shade of purple. This was a time before the olives – back when we were all better at pretending.

I was diving over and over again, trying to see how little of a splash I could make. Mom and Dad weren't talking, so everything was quiet except for the sound of the water. My skin got goosebumps while I walked up the ladder and to the end of the diving board. Then I would curl my toes around the edge of the board and grip it for a second before I bounced and dived.

I could see the dive in slow motion while I was in the middle of it. And then I could feel it in my bones as I entered the water – I knew if I should straighten my elbows or my right foot a second before I hit the water. Then there would be the perfect quiet of the dive and the rush of the water in my ears and finally up to the surface, tilting my head to let the water brush the hair from my face. I came up as quietly as I went in.

And then I came up from one dive and my parents were fighting. Really fighting, as in yelling at one another. Yelling good and loud for the first and only time I ever saw. Up until then everything had been silent. I remember thinking, So this is what all the waiting was for.

My dad threw his paper down on the patio table and said, 'If you would stop being a mannequin for just five seconds we might actually have ... '

Mom stopped worrying about her nails. Dad stood up. I made my way onto the diving board while my mother said, 'If you were actually what you claim to be – '

It was silent under the water. I sank down as far as I could go before I had to turn around and come up for breath.

The next dive was really good. The slow motion kicked in and I kept everything perfectly straight. There was hardly a wave, hardly a ripple, and then the silence where I could control everything.

I can't see myself in the future anymore. I can't see me doing anything at all. Nothing good anyway. And then I know. I'm so sure of what I know that I say it right out loud. 'Phillipina Morley, this has got to stop.' I say my name out loud for the first time in this little trailer and a bit of the nausea goes away. I lay my head against the cool of the table and close my eyes.

Things have been pretty rocky around the trailer lately. It seems like when one part of life comes loose then everything else starts to fall apart too.

The other night while I was lying on the couch, I figured out my strongest part. I got together all the things I like about myself – things like how I can be myself in every situation and how I'm mostly in a good mood, little things like that – and I dumped them in a big pile, and you know what they added up to? They said, *I like Hazel, no matter what*.

That's one thing I have that King doesn't. I know he loves me, and he loves his friends, and he loves having fun, but when it comes right down to it he doesn't love himself – he doesn't even like himself very much. If there were two Kings in this world they definitely wouldn't be friends, and they would probably beat the hell out of one another.

I keep thinking of all of our fun times, like at Old Joe's when King is the centre of attention and everyone loves him, especially me. Times when he's relaxed and happy and has no cares, that's King. And then there are the times when I climb into my bubble discoveries and he has to come and rescue me from myself. At those times, he's all white-knight sparkly, and that's King. When he's fixing a bike and he's doing a good job, that's King. And he used to be King when he was playing music, but that was before the anger started. But, like I say, when one thing starts to slide, so do others.

Today was my first day back at the thrift. The day was mostly okay except for just now when I got home. There was King. He was in the front yard, his bike tipped over, lying on its side in the wildflowers. He was kicking it, saying, 'You stupid useless piece of crap.'

There's not a thing in the world you can do with a situation like that, so I did a one-eighty and turned the Duster back towards the highway.

I could hear him swearing blocks away. He kept saying the same thing: 'stupid and useless' and 'useless and stupid.' King's strongest thing is to be King. King as other people see him – not as he really is.

I drive the Duster over to the other side of town and then out to the country roads – spirographing again. I'm tired of avoiding everything and tired of driving around in no direction, so I turn around and head back to the trailer. My leg is mostly better. After King left in a fury that night I lay on the couch for another four days – four days that I don't really remember going by.

And then Egg came to the trailer. He sat me up and brought me some food. He got me cleaned up and fed and feeling better and back to work. The good thing was all that not moving did wonders for my leg because when I saw Egg at the door, knocking and shyly peering through the screen, I walked over and welcomed him on my own two legs with hardly even a limp. It's not like I'm taking up hiking or anything, but all in all, I'm mostly better.

It feels really great to be out of the house and on my own steam again. It feels especially good to be driving the Duster, but my leg is starting to hurt a bit and I'm glad I'm almost home.

I park in the front yard beside where King is crouched over his bike. I'm careful not to stir up too much dust with my tires and piss King off all over again. He doesn't seem to notice that I'm back so I walk straight past him and sit on the front step. I wonder what he did those days I was on the couch. I wonder what he thought for those four days when I wasn't even eating.

He seems much calmer than before I went for the drive. For some awful reason I want that calm to shatter.

I sit and look around at nothing. Mostly, I'm trying to not look at King. I'm thinking about all the times I've sat right here on this step waiting for things to blow over. This makes me mad all over again. Sitting on a step talking down the night is okay, or sitting on a step watching the sun go down is okay, but sitting on a step because there's no other place for you in the whole wide world really sucks.

King is in the middle of the lawn where his bike fell. I can see where he trampled a bunch of the wildflowers to get them out of his way. One of the brake levers on the bike is bent and he's hammering it back into place.

Here's Hazel in her flower dress and her hair all done up, and she has nowhere to go. That's what I'm mad at. And it's all my fault. I did this to me.

'Hey, King,' I say. He doesn't answer, just keeps trying to fix his bike. I decide to try again. 'King, what's broken over there?'

He doesn't say anything. He doesn't even look up.

'Guess it's nothing then. Nope, nothing at all. I guess you're just fixing your bike for nothing.'

He looks me right in the eye for the first time in a long time and it makes the hair on the back of my neck stand up. 'Pretty damn pointless,' he says.

'What's pretty damn pointless?' I say and I look right back at him. I know I'm on thin ice but I can't stop myself.

He doesn't say anything, but he has stopped trying to fix the bike and I can see him thinking and tightening up.

'What's pretty damn pointless?' I repeat and I can feel the ice getting thinner.

King throws the wrench he's holding. 'You know what's pointless?' he says. 'Do you really want to know? This bike is pointless. This trailer is pointless. This whole damn thing is pointless!'

'Yeah, I guess so,' I say.

This stops him in mid-rant. I wasn't supposed to agree with him. But I can't make myself follow our usual routine anymore – it doesn't work. I have to push it, so maybe it will break and maybe, just maybe, we will find our strongest part.

I say, 'You're right. I can't disagree with you at all.'

King is lost now, floundering with the script change. 'What, Hazel? What do you want me to say?'

'I don't know, that's the thing. I have no idea what I want you to say. I was hoping you would come up with something.'

King stands straight and says, 'What the hell? Why are you on my back? Sometimes you make no sense.'

'Sometimes,' I say and drag out the word, 'sometimes you kick your bike just so you have to fix it again. And that – that makes no sense.'

Everything goes still. I never really appreciated the term 'wind going out of his sails' until I see King at this moment.

I'm thinking, *Laugh, King, this is when you laugh. This is when you laugh, and we talk and make everything better.*

If we broke down everything, dumped our scripts and started over, then we could navigate, watch for dust in the air and check the pressure in our tanks and do every little thing right. We could make it to the surface.

In my head I hear the voice-over from *The Six Million Dollar Man*: 'We can rebuild him.' And I want to say it out loud, to make King understand that there is a chance. For one second I am so hopeful that everything is going to change that I have the start of a smile on my lips just waiting for it. But instead I get, 'Fuck, Hazel, sometimes I really don't know who the hell you are.'

Before you rebuild, you have to get to the point where the rebuilding absolutely has to be done. If Steve Austin had survived his horrible accident with a limp instead of total paralysis he probably would have been happy with his old life and a cane.

King hauls his bike up, forgets about his broken brake lever and takes off. Just like that. Right down the road and out of the park. Dust blowing up behind him like in a cowboy movie. Everything but the setting sun.

King doesn't come back that evening or that night. First I was mad, and then I was worried. Now I'm neither. It's the next day, and I'm feeling peaceful, just bombing around the trailer doing a bit of reorganizing. It feels good, like finishing a puzzle. My leg is only a dull ache and I went to the hospital this morning to get the stitches out. The doctor said I was a remarkable healer. 'You don't know the half of it,' I told him.

I go over to Sissy's. 'Hey, Hazel,' she says.

'Hey,' I say. 'I hope that frying pan isn't handy.'

'Very funny,' she says, 'very funny, Hazel. You know, not everything in life is a joke. There are a lot of people who don't take things seriously and then they don't know how to handle themselves.'

'Okay, Sissy, I just thought I'd come over and see how you're doing.'

'Well, I'm fine,' she says. 'But I guess you're not so fine seeing how King took off and all that.'

'How do you know?'

'He came over here in the middle of the night and tried to get Spiney to go with him. He said he wanted to go up the coast. He said he couldn't get far enough fast enough. But Spiney didn't go because someone has to be at the shop. I don't see how King thinks he can – '

'Okay, Sissy,' I say, 'I just wanted to see that you were all right.'

'Of course I'm all right,' she says. 'Just because Spiney and me got in a little fight doesn't mean the whole world is coming to an end. Real people just get over that stuff, you know.'

Sometimes Sissy is just too much to deal with. Sometimes it's not one of her evil moods that's the problem, sometimes it's the truth that's the problem. She never learned how to sugar-coat anything.

I don't want to hear about what King said. And I don't want to hear that he said it to her and not to me. I can't remember if Sissy was always like this. I know that she is my friend, but to tell the truth, I don't really know why. I guess that's the kind of friendship that happens between neighbours.

The afternoon seems long. I try to think of what I would normally do at this time of day and realize that the answer is not much of anything. There always seems to be something to take care of or scuba lessons to study for or work to do, but today is open. Tomorrow is another day at the thrift, but today is all mine. Everything is full of possibility.

Back at the trailer, I crack a beer and spread out on a blanket in the front yard. I lie in the flowers, stare up at the sky and remember that this is the reason I grew the flowers in the first place. My whole plan was to lie here and look up at the sky through the flowers. I never do it, though, and I decide that from now on I'm going to do some wildflower lounging every day. I'm pencilling it in.

I sing a little song to myself about the flowers and think of what to do next. The singing feels great. It's been a long time since anything light and fun has come out of this set of vocal cords. I can feel the notes vibrate in my chest and bubble out into words. It goes like this so far: 'Singing to the weeds on a Tuesday, play with the light. Ain't it sweet to sleep in the afternoon? I never knew – I sure did like to be with you.' Well, it goes something like that anyway. I'm not done yet.

I squint and let the sun make patterns across my eyelashes. From my viewpoint the flowers tower up into the sky. I could be an ant or a little speck of dust. From here I could be anything in the world. Perspective is everything.

Then I realize that I haven't been listening for the sound of a motorbike. I haven't been waiting. For hours and hours I haven't been waiting.

If I lower my eyelids just the right way, I can see prism colours along my lashes. Sparkle and magic are in the eye of the beholder. Literally. It's in everything. Sometimes you just have to squint to see it.

Today Egg and I are back at the thrift. We're celebrating the fact that I got my scuba-diving licence. Egg brought cake in the shape of a goldfish – he made it himself.

'What are you doing for the next couple of weeks?'

'Nothing. I'm just waiting for school to start again, I guess.'

'Do you think you could mind the thrift for a while?'

'Do you have plans?'

'Sort of.'

'Details, please.'

'No details.'

'Stay just like that,' says Egg. He has a strange contraption in his hand. He holds it up. It's the leather-flask mystery item that he got from the thrift. That day seems like a million years ago. 'It turned out to be a camera,' he says and takes a picture. 'I guess I didn't get every camera in the place last year.'

'A Polaroid, cool.'

'The Polaroid Land Camera, to be exact,' he says and smiles.

And at the same time my brain takes a picture too: Egg with a big grin on his face, exploring the camera like it's a whole different world.

'Can I keep this?' He holds up the picture he just took.

'You bet. Egg?' I want to tell him everything but I can't seem to find a place to start.

'It's okay, Hazel,' he says. He takes one look at me and I know that he knows everything I have to tell him. 'Why don't I give you my address at school?' he says and writes on a piece of receipt paper. 'Just in case you want to send me a postcard or something.'

'Sounds good, Egg.' That's all I can manage to get out.

It's been nine days now, no phone call or anything.

Spiney is at the door. He's still in his work clothes and he's got his ball cap in his hands. When I look at him I feel like one of those wives who got the bad-news visits during war.

'What's up?' I say. 'You're looking guilty as hell.'

Spiney stops smiling. 'I thought I should tell you that he called.'

'Oh. Come on in. I was just hanging out. Want a beer?'

Spiney can never resist a beer, so he comes in and we sit at the kitchen table and cheers.

'This place looks really different,' he says.

'Yeah.' I look around. 'I guess it does. I just felt like a change.'

Spiney takes a long drink. 'Well, he called me at the shop today and asked if I wanted to take a trip.'

'Trips are good,' I say. I'm being cool, smiling and stealing one of Spiney's cigarettes, trying to look like nothing in the world could ever bother me.

'A long trip,' he says.

'Yep,' I say.

There's a lump in my throat, and I take another drink to swallow it away. Once I think I'm safe I say, 'Well, I guess I thought so.'

'You guys fight?'

'Kind of. There was a fight, but there were a lot of other things too.'

'There's always a lot of things,' Spiney says.

'Yeah, I guess there are. And sometimes all the little things point at the same big thing, you know?'

I stare at the ceiling.

'Did he sound okay?' I ask.

'Yeah.'

'Happy?'

Spiney won't meet my eyes and I can tell that he doesn't want to tell me that King sounded happy. He just shrugs.

'Happy,' I say and lean back in my chair. 'Well, Spiney, it looks as though I've been left.'

I try to smile, but this time I really do start to cry. It comes so fast that I can't hold it back and then it stops as soon as it started.

'Well,' Spiney says.

'Well,' I say. 'Want to play some crazy eights?'

'Sure.'

'Want some whisky?'

'You know it.'

So I get the bottle and the cards. We settle into a game, not really saying much of anything, just flipping the cards and playing. We finish the second game of crazy eights and switch to cribbage. I get out the crib board and lay it on the table.

'You're going to get your ass whooped,' I say.

'Not a hope in hell, Hazel.'

I skunk him right off the bat and the tournament is on. Spiney won't stop playing until he wins or until he loses so badly that he can't face another game.

'Are you and Sissy okay?' I ask.

'Back to normal.'

'And is that all right for you?'

'Sure.'

'I'm glad. Good for you.' We don't talk much while we play the first hand. Then I take a deep breath and say, 'I guess I know about King. I guess I knew all along.'

'What do you mean?' Spiney looks worried but tries to cover it with counting nine.

I lay a six. 'Fifteen for two,' I say. 'I guess it's like … I don't know … '

'Like what? Twenty-five.'

'Thirty. Well, when you think about you and Sissy, can you see you guys in a year from now?'

'Thirty-one. I guess.'

'Ten. Well, how about five years?'

'Fifteen for two. Yeah, sure.'

'Twenty-five. Well, lately I can't see next week most of the time.'

We count our points and Spiney says, 'Man, that's weird.'

'Yeah, I guess it is kind of weird.'

'I always thought you guys were happy. Your crib.'

'Yeah, we were. That's the thing.'

Spiney doesn't say anything for a while and then, 'Are you going to wait?'

I don't answer right away. In my head, I add up all the time I spent on the front step waiting for King to calm down or waiting for him to come home and all the time I spent waiting for him to want to be on the front step along with me. 'I guess I've waited long enough,' I say.

I count my points and Spiney shuffles for the next hand. 'You know, King's my best friend, and I hate to tell you this, but I feel like it's the right thing to do now that you've made up your mind. He's been … '

Spiney fumbles with the cards and I reach across the table to stop him from shuffling. 'Don't say it then, Spiney.'

'Yeah. Yeah, I guess I won't.'

'Besides … I know.'

'Yeah, I guess you do.'

Spiney lays the cards down on the table, puts his hands on my shoulders and looks straight at me, kind of smiling, kind of sad. He doesn't say anything, just sits there and shakes his head in that silent way he has of saying everything.

Then he kisses me on the forehead and walks out the front door. All I can do is stare at the door and nod my head, even long after it's closed.

I've got a hangover because Spiney and I got into the crib tournament of the universe last night. He's been over every night for the past three nights and I know that he's doing it just to keep me company. We don't talk about it, though.

I'm doing some wildflower lounging and letting my body get on with the healing process. I kind of like this lazy hangover state because you have no feeling like you should get up and do something. Total relaxation because everything hurts. I'm in a body coma.

I hear the motorbike right away. I hear it drive close and then stop. What has it been? Thirteen days? Fifteen? I can't really remember, but I knew it would be soon. I guess I was waiting after all.

And here he is, standing above me, in front of the sun. He's smiling that really great lopsided King smile and saying, 'Hangover?'

'You bet,' I say and move so he can sit on some of my blanket.

'It's nice here,' he says.

'Always was.'

'Guess so.'

I don't say anything because there's nothing to say. We just sit for a while. A long while. Long enough for me to be surprised when he finally says, 'Hazel, you're not useless.'

'I know.'

There's another long pause and then he says, 'There's this thing, this feeling that always bugs me. I keep wondering what I'm doing with myself.'

‘Everybody wonders about that sort of thing.’

‘It’s just that I get stuck on it, and I can’t seem to figure it out. Then I have to do something to get perspective. You know?’

‘Like what?’

‘Well, like my trip.’

‘I know. Your trip and your singing in the gravel pit and playing music like some evil creature and all the rest of the crazy things you do. So what perspective did you get this time?’

I lie still on the ground, feeling my breathing and the sun. I wait.

‘Well, I guess the perspective is that I love you.’

‘That’s it?’

‘Yeah, isn’t that enough?’

‘I thought so, but I guess it isn’t. Not really.’

‘Well, what is?’

‘That’s your own question,’ I say. ‘Not mine.’

‘Look, Hazel, I came here to make up. Why are you doing this?’

‘Because some things just aren’t good enough anymore.’

‘Aw, shit, come on. It’s the same as it always was.’

‘Yeah, that’s just it.’

King is about to say more but trails off and looks up at the sky.

I’m relaxed now. All the bad stuff is out. ‘See, King, there’s always going to be one more thing. I’m not all of it for you. I guess there’s one more thing for me too.’

‘Who is it?’

‘No one, just something else. A whole lot of something else.’

King stretches out beside me. We don’t touch. Time goes by.

'Long trip?' I ask.

'Yeah, lots of riding.'

'Was it good, though?'

'Yeah, mostly. It's really great to get out sometimes, you know? Sleeping in the rough and all that feels pretty good.'

King gets a couple of beers out of his backpack and passes one to me.

'Yeah, I was thinking of trying a bit of that myself,' I say and open the beer. I have to hold it away from me because it fizzes over my fingers. 'Yep,' I say, 'get out and around for a while.'

'Really?'

'Yeah, you know how I got my scuba licence?'

'Sure.'

'Well, I'm thinking of taking the Duster and heading south. Just see what happens. See where the drive takes me and then go diving.'

'Sounds wicked.'

'I'm hoping so. I'm going to sell the trailer. Want to buy it?'

We laugh, and King says, 'I don't know. I thought I had all my plans in you but now I guess I don't. I have some more thinking to do.'

'Don't worry, it will only take a long motorbike ride to figure it out,' I say and we laugh again.

'Too bad,' King says. He looks up at the sky and squints his eyes. 'Too bad,' he says again.

I get a lump in my throat and try to swallow it down with beer. 'Yeah, too bad,' I say.

'I guess we can't start over?' King says.

'I guess not.'

'Just thought I'd try.'

'Trying never hurt anyone,' I say. 'It's not the trying that gets you.'

'Ain't that the truth.'

And we just lie in the wildflowers. We don't have to say anything else. We don't have to talk at all, because that's the kind of people we are.

Acknowledgements

Much gratitude to Alana Wilcox, editor at Coach House Books, for finding a story within a mess of pages. All credit for this book is hers and all errors I claim as my own. To Christina Palassio and Evan Munday at Coach House for their unswerving dedication and endless hours of work. I don't know how you do it! And to Carolyn Swayze for her compassion, her excitement and her faith.

And of course to my friends, family and mentors for every single thing in this big fantastic world: Bill Arab, Dana Boettger, Sheila Braam of Sheila Braam Photography, Christine Cleghorn, Michele Desmarais, fellow UBC students, Olivier Grard, Christine Haley, Ron Haney, Christine Harrington, Catherine Hayday, Cathy Helbig, Adrian Jones, Tommy Krowski, George McWhirter, Kathryn Mockler, MyJellybean.com, John Newton, Ontario Arts Council, Pan on the Danforth, James Peters, Kim and Gord Sauder, Ann Marie Sluga, Cynthia Smith, *This* magazine, Peggy Thompson, the University of British Columbia, and, to Joe and Sheila Voisin, all my love and gratitude.

About the Author

TANYA CHAPMAN is a graduate of the UBC creative writing program. Her short story 'Spring the Chick' won *This* magazine's Great Canadian Literary Hunt. She has had two short films produced and the Ontario Arts Council has supported her new manuscript, *The Welcoming Place*. She works as the director of communications at the Directors Guild of Canada in Ontario.

Typeset in CC Galliard with Linoscript
printed and bound at the Coach House on bpNichol Lane,
September 2006.

Edited and designed by Alana Wilcox
Author photo by Sheila Braam of Sheila Braam Photography

Coach House Books
401 Huron Street on bpNichol Lane
Toronto, Ontario M5S 2G5
Canada

416 979 2217
800 367 6360

mail@chbooks.com
www.chbooks.com